I0733484

The Look of Love

Aloha Romance Series ✥ Book Five

CHRIS KENISTON

Indie House Publishing

MORE BOOKS
By Chris Keniston

Hart Land
Heather
Lily
Violet
Iris
Hyacinth
Rose
Calytrix
Zinnia
Poppy
Picture Perfect

Farraday Country
Adam
Brooks
Connor
Declan
Ethan
Finn
Grace
Hannah
Ian
Jamison
Keeping Eileen
Loving Chloe
Morgan
Neil

Honeymoon Series
Honeymoon for One
Honeymoon for Three
Honeymoon for Four
Honeymoon for Five

Aloha Romance Series:
Aloha Texas
Almost Paradise
Mai Tai Marriage
Dive Into You
Look of Love
Love by Design
Love Walks In
Shell Game
Flirting with Paradise

Surf's Up Flirts:
(Aloha Series Companions)
Shall We Dance
Love on Tap
Head Over Heels
Perfect Match
Just One Kiss
It Had to Be You
Cat's Meow

ACKNOWLEDGEMENTS

In an effort to write faster I am very thankful for all the friends who come to my aid in so many different ways. But I have to give a special thank you to:

Kathy Ivan, Linda Steinberg and the rest of the Plotting Princesses for always pointing me in the right direction. Cheryl Lucas for being the best sounding board and idea person around—any time of day or night. And of course my family who still smile and nod when I say "sorry, I'm on deadline."

CHAPTER ONE

"**R**emind me again why we're here three hours before departure?" Madeleine Harper tugged at the handle on the last of her mother's three suitcases and thanked heaven for whoever invented four-wheeled luggage. The new spinner style suitcases made juggling all these bags and her carryon so much easier. For the last couple of days she'd watched her mother flutter from baby boutique to mega–box store like a merrily drunken butterfly. Now they were hauling her loot to Nick's house in Kona.

"Your mother is anxious to get to Hawaii." Randy Harper relieved his daughter of the two larger suitcases. "And just in case every baby shop on the Big Island has gone out of business, she's bringing enough merchandise for a tribe of grandchildren."

"Not everything is for the new baby." Yvette Harper tapped her toe, waiting for her husband to catch up. "There's plenty here for Bradley too."

"Of course." Madeleine took a deep breath and followed her parents into the terminal at LAX. She was just as excited about her brother, Nick's, soon-to-arrive second child, especially since she'd not met her nephew Bradley until he was almost six. But she'd have also been just as happy to sleep in an extra hour this morning rather than arrive at the airport at the crack of dawn only to hurry up and wait.

"Good grief." Maddie stopped short at the maze of passengers ahead. "Is that the security line?"

Like a matched set of bobbleheads, Yvette and Randy Harper scanned the crowd from one side of the cavernous airport to the other and nodded. "Looks like it."

"Maybe arriving insanely early wasn't such a bad idea after all." Madeleine tightened her grip on each suitcase, and, like an obedient duckling, followed single file behind her parents. She was nearly to the ticketing area when one of the wheels on her mom's trunk-size suitcase went rogue. The fifty-pound bag veered suddenly right and slammed into the passenger backing away from a self-check kiosk. "Oh, I'm so sorry." Mortification erupted at the sight of the wayward bag bouncing off the back of denim-clad legs.

A six-foot wall of a man turned and glanced down dismissively at the offending suitcase she'd already managed to corral back to her side. "No problem."

Sea green eyes with fine laugh lines stretching from the corners stared down at her, and Madeleine was sure what little saliva was left in her mouth had just turned to dust. Reflexively she took a step back. Not till her knees buckled beneath her and her arms flew up in an effort to regain her balance, did she remember the other bag still parked at her feet. Squealing like a young girl spotting a mouse, she thrust her arms backward in a flimsy effort to break her fall when two large vises tightened around her forearms.

"Easy there."

His deep, slow, even tone brought a wave of instant calm.

Steady on her feet again, she managed an appreciative smile. "Thanks."

"Any time." His hands hovered in midair as he retreated, no doubt concerned she might find something else to topple over.

"There you are." Randy Harper appeared beside his daughter. "I thought you were right behind me."

"I was. I am." She reached for the two bags, spinning the troublesome one to the other side and looked up at the stranger she'd collided with. "Thank you again."

"You're welcome, and remember next time to signal before turning." With a short nod and a broad smile he turned on his heel and headed toward security.

Randy repositioned himself beside his daughter, taking

control of one of the bags. "What was that all about?"

"Nothing much." Maddie maneuvered the bulky bag forward. "I accidentally plowed into him with Mom's suitcase."

"Considering how overloaded these suckers are, you're lucky he didn't break a leg."

"At least now if anyone tries to sue, we have a great lawyer in the family." As if on cue, her cell phone rang. Apparently she wasn't the only one up insanely early this morning. Rummaging through her purse, she pulled out her phone. Grinning like a schoolgirl, she answered with a syrupy "Aloha."

"Try not to sound so glum," her brother, Nick, teased.

"Are you kidding? A whole month without my phone ringing every five minutes, no clients expecting me to go running when they find the perfect house on the Internet, even if it doesn't have a single one of their must-have items, and no arrogant coworkers thinking they're God's gift to women—"

"I detect a story there."

Nick was the best big brother a girl could ask for. When she was really young and her ice cream would fall off the cone, which seemed to happen to her a lot, he'd always shared his. In junior high a couple of creepy teens had followed her and her friend around at the movie theater, and then taken a seat beside her. When she'd called Nick in a panic, he'd left a party to sit with her and then drive her home. And on her sixteenth birthday he'd come home from A&M and taught her how to drink smart, insisting no one would take advantage of his little sister by getting her drunk. She'd missed him horribly while he was at school and even more when he'd left for active duty. When he'd finally separated from the navy a few years ago, she'd hoped he'd settle down near her in San Diego, but, if she had to visit her brother somewhere, she was delighted he'd moved to Hawaii and not South Dakota.

"No story," she answered, "just another idiot at the office who looks good on the surface and turns out to be an immature dud." For the next thirty days Maddie was going to be on the first real vacation she'd had since college. No work. No hassles. No men.

Daniel O'Neil shoved his carry-on into the overhead bin. One of the many things he'd learned after twenty years in the navy was how to pack an overnight seabag to last a week. When first asked to speak at the explosive ordinance disposal symposium, he'd been reluctant to participate. Then he'd learned the venue would be Honolulu. No way would he turn down an easy excuse to pop over and check up on Carolyn's new home.

All he had to do was survive the six hour long flight in seats designed for pygmies. At least now most airlines offered an upgrade with enough legroom to keep him from having to fly with his knees knocking the seat in front of him. Of course, with or without legroom, flying commercial beat flying halfway around the world on a military transport.

Strapped in, Daniel pulled out the latest John Grisham novel, and cell phone in hand, swiped at the screen to flip it to airplane mode when Carolyn's ring tone sounded. "O'Neil here."

"Civilians usually answer with *hello*." Amusement carried in her voice.

"Hello," he repeated more warmly. Dan was still getting used to being a civilian. And having a daughter. "All settled in?"

"And loving it. There really is no place like paradise. But I've saved a few little things for you to do." She paused a moment. "That is if you don't mind, I mean. You are pretty handy?"

"I am, and I'm happy to help." *Handy* was a rather loose-fitting handle for an EOD technician. Most of them could put MacGyver to shame. In order to safely disarm explosive devices of any shape or size, in any location, or under any circumstances, it was a given he and his men qualified as *handy*. "I should be finished with business in time for a late flight to Kona day after tomorrow. I'll call and confirm." Not that he hadn't timed his schedule to the minute already.

"Okay. See you then. ... Bye."

"See you day after tomorrow." For a few long seconds after the call disconnected, he stared at the screen. How differently would their conversation have gone if he'd been her dad her whole life and not just the father she'd tracked down less than a year ago?

"Can't wait to see you, Daddy."

"Me too, princess."

"I love you."

"I love you more."

Changing the appropriate settings, he slid the phone into his briefcase and returned to the paperback. Maybe a legal thriller would get his mind off the choices he'd made in his life. And the ones on his plate now.

"Excuse me." The soft, slightly southern and somewhat familiar voice caught his attention.

Looking up from his book, he saw the young brunette who had slammed her luggage into him and then had nearly taken a dive over the same suitcases. Standing in the aisle, she juggled a hardcased carryon while trying not to assault every passenger within five feet of her.

"Leave it in your seat, and I'll put it up for you." The instructions came from the same older gentleman who had come looking for her in the terminal. Possibly her father, possibly her companion.

With shoulder-length chestnut hair and big brown eyes that danced with a love of life, she was definitely pretty enough to be a trophy wife but didn't have any other characteristics of a woman marrying for money or social position. Setting aside his book, he pushed to his feet, carefully ducking to avoid slamming his head on the bins. "Allow me." Dan had to bite back a smile at the way her eyes rounded with surprise and her cheeks flushed with color.

She eased back to hand the bag to him and stepped on

the foot of the person behind her. "Oh, I'm so sorry," she turned, apologizing to the petite woman.

Dan shoved the carry-on between a backpack and his bag and, slamming the lid to the full compartment shut, returned to his window seat.

The still blushing brunette slid into the spot beside him, and then, shimmying back and forth in place searching for the seat belt, she yanked hard at the strap underneath her. With the extra effort, her arm came flying back and only his well-honed reflexes prevented him from getting smacked in the face. No, she was definitely not a trophy wife.

Once again opening his book, he turned his attention to the plot and did his best to ignore the young thing settling in beside him. When the captain announced over the loud speaker that they were next in line and would be taking off any minute, he noticed she leaned her head back and closed her eyes. *Afraid of flying?*

"No, not really."

When she turned to face him, he realized he'd actually given voice to his thoughts. He had no business chatting up the lady. She probably wasn't much older than Carolyn. Then again, conversing with your seatmate wasn't necessarily a precursor to a torrid affair. Once off the airplane, he had no reason to ever see the girl again in his life. And even if he were tempted by the mild floral perfume she wore or the cute way her cheeks kept flushing with embarrassment, highlighting porcelain-perfect skin, he'd only be in Honolulu for a day and a half. "There's really nothing to it."

"I know." She sighed. "It's just the takeoff and landing that reminds me of all the things that could go wrong."

This was probably not the time to point out all the things that could go wrong in between takeoff and landing. "We'll be up in the air in no time."

Her head bobbed. "You fly a lot?"

"Used to."

"For work?"

This time he was the one to nod.

"Salesman?"

"Navy."

"Really?" Her face brightened, and she shifted to better face him. She had a captivating smile that he found way more appealing than he should. "My brother was in the navy. How long have you been out?"

He could almost count the time down to the minutes. "Going on thirty days."

"That would explain the haircut."

He resisted the urge to rake his hand across his hairline. "Some habits are hard to break."

"You don't need to. The military cut looks good on you. Shows off your eyes."

Was she flirting with him? "Thank you."

"So what brings you to Hawaii?"

"I'm giving a speech at a symposium."

"Anything interesting?"

"I doubt it." He didn't know many women who wanted to know the ins and outs of blowing things up for a living. EOD techs had almost as high a divorce rate as the SEALs. But he wasn't in EOD anymore. He wasn't responsible for men's lives. For a country's safety. There would be no more moving from base to base, pulling out on missions to undisclosed locations for an undisclosed amount of time. And no excuses for not settling down to a normal family life.

On the other hand he'd spent the last thirty days living normal. For him. He still woke up at 5:30. Still made his bed with hospital corners. And still couldn't bring himself to put his hands in his pockets. Maybe leaving the navy to start his life over wasn't the best idea he'd ever had.

CHAPTER TWO

66 "What are you doing?" Nick Harper walked into the guest room in time to find his very pregnant wife wrestling a mattress.

"The package said suitable for pillowtop beds." She tugged at a corner and grunted. "They lied."

"Let me." He settled his hands over hers, gently nudging them away. "Please."

Inhaling a deep breath, Kara straightened. Hands on her lower back, she bowed slightly backward before grabbing the flat sheet.

Having successfully tucked the fitted corners over the new mattress, Nick held his hand out to his wife. "I can do that."

"So can I." She flicked the sheet from the corners and let the large swath of fabric settle over the bed. "I'm not an invalid."

Kara had said that very phrase to him and others so many times over the last few months it should be etched on his eardrums. But he couldn't help fussing over her. He had no idea it was possible to love and worry so much about another person. But he simply couldn't fathom his world without Kara in it. "It's my family. I should have bed-making duty."

Rolling her eyes, Kara smoothed out the sheet and reached for a lightweight coverlet. "If you're so eager to help, grab a corner."

The bed made and the decorative pillows in place, Nick swirled his wife into his arms. "Have I mentioned lately how much I love you, Mrs. Harper?"

Chuckling softly, Kara leaned into the embrace. "Feel

free to remind me again."

"I think I will." Pulling her closer, he let his lips settle on hers. He didn't think he'd ever grow tired of kissing this woman. A hard thump from her belly whacked him in the side. He broke off the kiss with a smile. "Today it feels like you're nurturing a future middle linebacker."

"And here I was thinking a gymnast."

Together they had decided to do things the old-fashioned way and not be told the sex of the baby. Letting his hand settle over her tummy around the spot that had kicked him, he waited. By now Kara knew the routine and patiently waited with him for Baby H to either settle down or move again for his or her daddy. More often than not the baby would cooperate and roll under the warmth of his palm. Which was one of the many reasons he actually thought maybe this child was a little girl, trying very successfully to wrap Daddy around her finger.

"There she goes." Nick lowered his lips to within inches of his wife's rounded tummy. "Pretty soon your gramma and grampa and aunt Maddie will be landing in Kona. They're coming just to meet you."

"Which reminds me. The furniture store called this morning, and the new sofa bed won't be delivered until Friday."

"Why?" Nick straightened.

"The man spoke to me for almost twenty minutes, apologizing profusely, but never did get around to giving me an explanation that might stand up in a court of law."

"Daddy?" Bradley Harper walked into the guest room. "Is Gramma almost here?"

"Not quite, sport." Nick hunched down in front of his son. "She and Grampa and Aunt Maddie aren't coming until dinnertime."

"Can we have dinner early?"

Nick smothered a laugh at his son's logic. "That won't get Gramma and Grampa here any earlier than 6:30."

"Oh. Okay." The curly haired little boy's face went from resignation to delight in a flash. "Do I still get to share my room with Aunt Maddie?"

"You sure do," Kara chimed in, wrapping her arms around the little boy.

It was hard for Nick to believe that, a couple of years ago, he was a single guy going through the motions of a carefree life. The playboy living over the Surf's Up Saloon seemed a lifetime ago. After all, what more could a guy ask for in life? A terrific wife, a sweet son, a baby on the way, and a best friend for a business partner who he'd trust with his life. His cell phone rang out, and Billy Everrett's name appeared. Nick had to smile. Sometimes his partner's timing was almost eerie. If Nick didn't know better, he'd be willing to bet the guy could read minds. "Hey."

"You ready for the deluge of relatives?" Laughter tickled Billy's words.

"You bet. Even ordered a new sofa bed for when Kara's aunt arrives in a couple of weeks."

"If she'd prefer, the offer still stands. Anyone who wants to bunk in a real bed can stay in one of our extra rooms."

"Appreciate it, man. Will let you know." Nick followed Kara and Bradley out of the bedroom. "So what's up?"

"Just got off the phone with Mom. She's decided she wants to have your family over for a little get-together before the baby comes."

"Uh-oh. How little is she thinking?"

"Just a few close friends." Amusement continued to resonate in Billy's voice.

"In other words, all of Kona?"

This time Billy chuckled loudly. "Probably."

"At least your mom is the best cook this side of the international date line."

"That she is."

"I'd better warn my sister to steer clear of any single men at the party in case your mom gets any funny ideas."

"It could be worse. You could have a brother for Mom to match up with Sara Alani."

"True. Though I don't understand why Sara can't seem to find a nice guy on her own."

"Might have something to do with the fact that she's not looking."

Nick laughed. "There is that."

"Anyhow, keep Saturday afternoon open. Mom insists next weekend is going to be too late."

Even though his business partner had no way of seeing him, Nick shook his head at Maile Everrett's timetable. Kara wasn't due for another three weeks, and the obstetrician, who to Nick looked older than dirt, insisted first babies are rarely in a hurry to meet the world.

One of the disadvantages of waking up in the middle of the night to catch a plane is that the odds of falling asleep during flight increase exponentially for every predawn hour that someone has been awake. An especially unfortunate result if the person sitting next to you turns out to be both nice and interesting.

Learning the handsome stranger beside her had recently separated from the navy had certainly explained a lot. From his stoic expression when Maddie had let the luggage plow into him, to his fast reflexes when she'd almost fallen head-over-suitcases. And of course, his chivalrous display when she couldn't quite manage to get her carry-on over her head without knocking into the backs of a few seats. But she'd wanted to learn more. She hadn't noticed any jewelry, so he wasn't a ring knocker. Nothing could separate a military academy graduate from his ring. She couldn't put her finger on why she knew, but she would bet her next commission check he had most definitely been an officer. And a mighty good-looking one at that.

When he'd stopped her from falling flat on her keister back in the terminal, Maddie got a long look into his eyes. Shades of river green, with tiny flecks of gold that shimmered when he smiled. If he were a bit younger, she would have asked if he knew her brother. Or any of Nick's friends. But even if he weren't at least a few years older than Nick, the fact that there were easily over a quarter of a million active-duty sailors in the US Navy made the odds of her seatmate and her brother knowing each other about par with the chance of her winning the lottery.

Maddie had hoped to find out more about him, starting with his name, but the wheels of the jetliner had barely left the tarmac when her eyelids grew heavy, and she dozed off. The sound of the captain's voice announcing the flight's descent into Honolulu woke her. Mr. Good-Looking Former Navy had his nose in a paperback. She didn't see that very often anymore. Most everyone she knew read on some sort of electronic device. Not this guy. Apparently a true traditionalist. Probably had the newspaper delivered to his front doorstep and kept a landline in the kitchen.

"Flight attendants prepare for landing." The captain's voice filled the aircraft.

She hadn't meant to stare at the man beside her, but she noticed his hands as he slipped a bookmark between the pages, closed the cover and dropped the book into the briefcase at his feet. Long slender fingers stretched out from a solid square palm. Nimble fingers. Maddie wondered if his job had required him using his hands. Her brother had strong hands with long fingers as well. He'd needed plenty of dexterity for what he'd done for Uncle Sam. She didn't want to even consider how often his fine motor skills might have saved his life.

"Sleep well?"

"Oh." Maddie rolled her neck left then right. "Yeah. I can't believe I slept for almost six hours."

"You must have needed it."

Just then the engine made an odd whirring noise as the ground, visible through the window, grew closer to the plane. Her accelerated pulse pounded in her ears. If taking off left her uneasy, landing wasn't any better.

"I'm the same way. If a man can sleep in troop seats, he can sleep anywhere."

Her fingers curling around the armrests, she blinked, then turned her attention from the window to the man sitting beside it. "I'm sorry. What did you say?"

The wheels hit the runway, the brakes squealing like a scared pig. Her hold on the armrest tightened.

"You can relax your grip before you break the chair." Just like at the terminal when he'd caught her by the arm to steady her, his low, deep voice wrapped her in a soothing sense of calm.

Easing her grasp, she lifted her hands and wiggled her fingers. If his gentle tone hadn't already been enough to make her relax, the lopsided grin that met her gaze when she looked up at him would have most definitely done the trick. That smile was incredibly disarming. For a short moment she wondered if the navy had been smart enough to use this man as a secret weapon. Of course that would only work if the enemy were a battalion of women. "I suspect this seat has survived worse."

His mouth lifted in a full-impact smile, and she had a sudden vision of this guy wearing dress whites and beating the ladies off with a club. He probably had several women in every port. Not that it was any of her business.

The plane rolled to a stop, and, like ants whose hill had been kicked over, the passengers stood and busied themselves, opening the overhead bins and gathering their belongings, preparing to escape the moment the single-file line of passengers forming in the aisle advanced.

"Is this your last stop?" he asked as she pushed to her feet, crouching under the low-hung ceiling.

"No, just a stopover." The man beside her stepped into the aisle, and she reached for the overhead bin.

"If you'll wait for me, I'll be happy to get your bag down for you."

Her first instinct was to politely refuse. After all, she'd successfully deplaned from plenty of flights without any help before, but then those emerald-green eyes twinkled at her, and she bobbed her head. "Thank you."

"My pleasure." The heart-stopping smile returned, and Maddie found herself thinking she'd gladly endure another six hours of flight anytime if she'd be confined next to this man.

CHAPTER THREE

Delayed. Not the words Maddie had wanted to hear. A scheduled three-hour layover was already too long. According to the flight information board, she and her parents now had five hours to sit and wait for the connecting flight to Kona.

"We might as well get out and do something. It's the middle of the afternoon on a beautiful day in paradise." Yvette Harper rubbed her hands together and, sporting a bright smile, looked from her husband to Maddie. "I vote for Pearl Harbor."

Randy Harper nodded at his wife. "I wonder if we could find a Hawaii Five-O tour?"

"What?" Accompanied by a hand on her hip, Yvette's smile gave way to buckled brows. This was one of the rare occasions when she didn't follow her husband's train of thought.

"All the places they show in the opening scenes of the TV show. We don't have to be at the gate for four hours. I bet we could fit both in."

"If it includes the new Steve McGarrett, I'm in." Maddie gave her dad a thumbs-up. She didn't have to worry about TV hunks turning into jerks. "I'll phone Nick and give him an update."

"Okay then." Yvette hefted her handbag higher on her shoulder and glanced at the overhead signs.

Randy held out his free hand to his wife, his fingers curling automatically around hers. "Taxis are that way."

Cell phone at her ear, Maddie followed behind her parents. Except for a stretch of time during her teenage years when she was absolutely mortified by her parents' public displays of affection, she loved how close her mom and dad were. She also found it downright eerie the way they so often spoke without saying a word. Most of the time she doubted anyone else in the world had that kind of relationship. Or that she'd ever find anything even close to it. But then she'd watch her brother and his wife, and, even though they didn't have the silent communication thing going, they certainly had the loving support down pat.

"I see you landed on time." On the other end of her call, Nick hadn't bothered with *hello*.

"For all the good it's doing us. The connecting flight is delayed."

"Why?"

"According to the gate agent when we landed, wherever the plane is now, it's having mechanical issues, and they're waiting for a different airplane."

"I suppose this is where 'better safe than sorry' fits. What's the new ETA?"

"Estimated arrival time is now 8:45 p.m."

"Bummer."

"Totally. We're going to do a little sightseeing. This is Mom's chance to finally see Pearl Harbor. We'll keep you posted with any updates."

"I'll try to keep Bradley from jumping out of his skin. He's so ready to see his gramma and grampa he's practically bursting at the seams. On the bright side he'll love getting to wait up past his bedtime."

"That's my night owl. Takes after his aunt Maddie. Give him a kiss from all of us, and we'll see you soon."

As Maddie slipped her phone into her purse, her father paused at an information kiosk with pamphlets on Honolulu tourist sights. Her mother quickly perused and sorted through what would be of most interest to everyone. Even though Maddie knew her mom really wanted to see Pearl Harbor, she also knew her mother would make sure that her husband got to see what he wanted as well. The woman was a stickler for having her family's back. And both Maddie and her dad knew that, if choices had to be made, Yvette Harper would always put her family first.

Maddie's mom handed her father two brochures, and, once again, the silent communication was on. Taking hold of them, he glanced at the covers, nodded at his wife then made his way to the cabstand. With their carry-ons safely tucked away in the trunk, her dad in the front seat, and she and her mom in the back, they were on their way to Pearl Harbor.

Fifteen minutes later the driver pulled up to the memorial park entrance. "Like I said before, at this time of day there won't be any tickets left for the memorial. Are you sure you don't want me to wait here for you while you go check?"

"No thank you." Randy Harper paid the driver. "Even if we can't go to the memorial, we can still pay our respects."

The guy shrugged and circled the car to unload the bags, set the two small carry-ons in front of him, then pointed to a building off to his right. "You'll find where to check these into a locker over there."

Maddie scanned the general area where the man had pointed, noticing the well-marked building. "Why don't you go see about tickets, and I'll check the bags."

With a nod her dad hurried across the way to the ticket booth while she and her mom secured a rented locker for all their bags. By the time they were settled in, her father approached them, shaking his head. "Cab driver was right. Not a chance. The clerk was very apologetic. She explained most tours are sold out by early morning, but we can still see the other museums. She was pretty sure getting into the USS *Bowfin* and maybe even the USS *Missouri* on Ford Island wouldn't be a problem."

Yvette Harper smiled at her husband before her gaze settled on the white memorial in the distance. "That will be lovely. Let's start with the *Bowfin*."

Not far from the locker rental area, the three waited with the other visitors, tickets and headgear in hand to tour the WWII submarine. A handful of people lined up behind them, and then a young man waved them on. From the deck of the submarine Maddie had a clear view of the USS *Arizona* memorial behind the submarine. "Mom, stand over here with Dad, and I'll take your picture."

Backing up to the metal railing, Randy and Yvette posed, both sporting broad grins.

"Oh, look." Yvette pointed over the side of the boat. "The fish are eating the barnacles."

Maddie hadn't cared much about the submarine, but her mother's love of everything navy thanks to her son and a canceled TV show about the JAG Corps was contagious. Inside the submarine's cramped quarters her mom smiled and giggled and compared different areas to scenes from her favorite show and seemed unusually concerned with all the brass on the ship. "Who do you think polishes all this?"

Everything on the sub was so compact, Maddie couldn't begin to imagine living here for months at a time. On TV and in movies, submarines didn't seem so small. Suddenly her cramped apartment in San Diego felt like a palace. Her father was especially fascinated with the details of the boat known as the Pearl Harbor Avenger.

Done with the preprogrammed tour, they hurried off the submarine to purchase tickets for the *Missouri*. Maddie paused to snap another photo. "Mom, Dad, hang on. Smile." Backing up, she tried to get her parents and the side of the *Bowfin* into the frame when she slammed into a warm wall and lost her balance.

Strong hands circled her arms, steadying her. Teetering in place, she spun about, her nose against rows of ribbons and medals. *Crap.* "My apologies, sir."

"The name's Daniel, and I thought we agreed you were going to use turn signals from now on?"

When Dan had stopped at his hotel and changed into his uniform in order to join the other symposium members for a barge tour at Pearl Harbor, the last person he'd expected to run into, literally, was the young brunette with a balance problem.

"I thought you said you'd left the navy."

With his fingers still folded around her slender arms, the urge to hang on startled him. "I have." He loosened his hold on her. "But less than eighty days out, I'm considered on terminal leave and technically still active duty."

"Oh." Taking a half step back, she scanned his chest and quickly read his insignia. "Captain?"

"Daniel O'Neil, at your service."

Her fingers lingered on his chest for a few more seconds, and the heat seeping through made him want to reach out and hold her again. And if the dazed gleam in her eye was any indication, she'd felt the sensation too. Having inched away, she stood beside her parents who had come across the walkway to meet them, the corners of her lips turned up in a smile. "Look who I found."

The older couple grinned up at him, but the father came closer, extending his hand. "How nice to see you again."

"Same here, but didn't your daughter tell me that you were catching a connecting flight in Honolulu?"

"We are." The man smiled. "But there was a delay, so we thought we'd take advantage of the extra time and pop over to Pearl Harbor and the *Arizona*."

Were they insane? People didn't just *pop over* to a major world tourist attraction between flights. Especially one known for never-ending lines and hours-long waits.

The woman beside him looked up at Dan with a toothpaste-commercial-worthy grin in place. "We were just on our way to the *Missouri*. Would you care to join us?"

Right about now, spending the remainder of the afternoon with three people whose names he didn't even know held a great deal more appeal than following his carefully laid-out schedule for the day. Including a two-hour boat tour with a bunch of sailors and bigwigs. Though, if he were honest with himself, the appeal all rested with the pretty brunette. One he had no business paying any attention to. She looked to be close to Carolyn's age. Which meant he was probably old enough to be her father—or darn close. "Thank you. I wish I could, but I'm expected to join my fellow speakers for a remembrance tour."

"Remembrance tour?" the brunette repeated.

"Afternoon tours offered for active-duty military or veterans and, in this case, for the benefit of those organizing and attending the symposium I'm speaking at tomorrow."

"How nice. Will you be seeing the *Missouri*?"

"No, ma'am. We'll be touring the boathouse museum, then watching a movie on the attack of Pearl Harbor, before visiting Ford Island and the USS *Arizona* Memorial."

"Well," the mother said wistfully, "maybe we'll run into you again anyhow."

Dan nodded, comfortable with his hands behind his back. "Perhaps we'll cross paths at the *Arizona*."

"No," the daughter supplied. "They were sold out by the time we got here."

He wasn't surprised. Not everyone was a planner like him. Some people enjoyed living life by the seat of their pants. But twenty years of naval discipline didn't leave much room for spontaneity. At the hotel he'd run into Admiral Wingate and his wife, and she'd carried on about how fortunate he and the other guests were to be able to participate in the special afternoon tour. Dan wished there was some way he could invite these folks to join him, but his chance to include guests had come and gone since he had first received the invitation.

"There you are." Admiral Wingate and his wife approached with two other officers.

"Admiral." He came to attention, noticing the brunette's eyes widen.

"As you were. I see your family decided to join you after all."

"No, sir. I didn't sign up for guests."

"Well, I'm sure we can accommodate them anyway. There wasn't a full barge to begin with, and Captain Alger's flight's been delayed, so he won't be joining us."

"Absolutely." The admiral's rotund wife reached out to the brunette's mother. "Too many men on this trip."

"Oh," the woman started, "I don't think—"

"If you don't mind giving up the *Missouri* to see the *Arizona*, it would be my pleasure to have you join us." Dan was addressing the parents, but it was purely selfish of him to want to get to visit more with the young lady. And if nothing else learn her name.

The mother glanced at the father, the man blinked, the wife smiled broadly, then facing her daughter, she asked, "Is that okay with you?"

"Of course." Maddie's response, though exuberant on the outside, felt less than sincere. He suspected that had more to do with his participation than a lack of eagerness to make her mother happy.

"Excellent." Admiral Wingate bobbed his head and turning on his heel; he and his wife led the way.

Dan extended his elbow for the brunette to take and leaned over slightly. "Since we are apparently now related, I should probably know your name."

"Madeleine." Slowly her fingers looped inside his elbow. "These are my parents, Randy and Yvette Harper."

"A pleasure," the two chorused.

"The pleasure is all mine." And he meant it. Winging it wasn't part of his nature, but this time he was pleased with the outcome. Very pleased.

Walking a few feet ahead of her parents, Madeleine lowered her voice. "Thank you very much for doing this. My mother doesn't fuss much, but I knew she was badly disappointed she wouldn't get to see the memorial close up."

"The *Arizona*?"

She nodded. "My brother served in the navy for over ten years, so Mom is extremely aware of how many mothers never got their sons back. Especially in the days when so many brothers served on the same ships."

"Yes. Twenty-three sets of brothers died that day on the *Arizona*." He didn't have to mention the date; it was understood.

"How awful."

All he could do was nod. There wasn't much else to say. War was hell. No one would argue that point. And especially not him.

CHAPTER FOUR

addie had no idea how she'd wound up on a private navy barge with more officers than she'd ever seen in one place before, but she couldn't imagine a better way to view the memorial. Facts and figures were flying. Many of the men had served at Pearl at some point in their navy careers. A few were currently stationed on base. But all had paid their respects at one time or another.

Between the short film and the ongoing conversations among the passengers, she was overrun with details. Many things she'd already learned: it's a living memorial, the final resting place of the souls lost onboard that day. What she hadn't known previously was that the ship had been leaking oil on a daily basis since December 7, 1941. She'd felt the sting of tears herself when Admiral Wingate had explained that every bead of oil that seeped from the wreckage—known as the *black tears*—is considered the USS *Arizona* weeping for her dead.

Buoys floating near the memorial marked the forward and aft ends of the ship. Maddie thought of her brother when she heard that every year a memorial service is held for the *Arizona* survivors who had chosen, upon their deaths years later, to be buried with their shipmates. She made a mental note to ask Nick if he'd ever been one of the navy divers to deposit the urn of those sailors' cremated remains beneath one of the *Arizona*'s gun turrets. As an EOD tech she didn't think he would have done that duty, but he *was* a navy diver.

Apparently active-duty servicemen are expected to visit the memorial in uniform. Which explained why Dan had changed after his flight. Summer whites for the navy. No BDUs. Respect was key. And fortunately most of the tourists felt the same way. A regular tourist ferry docked at the opposite edge of the memorial at the same time as their barge. Cameras and phones clicked away as folks debarked. The moment they rose to the entrance to the memorial, cameras stilled; voices quieted. The pain and shock of the events and losses all those decades ago weighed heavily on every visitor. Maddie wasn't normally a fan of modern architecture, but the bright white structure straddling the sunken vessel seemed the perfect fit for combining sorrow and hope.

The most unexpected happening for Maddie came from a Japanese couple who didn't appear to speak much English. As they read the names on the memorial wall of the lives lost and then looked about, Maddie noticed a tear slip from the corner of the woman's eye. Turning as Maddie and Dan crossed the couple's path, both bowed and whispered, "So very sorry."

The knot that had lived in Maddie's stomach all the years her brother had served his country took up momentary residence once again. She'd never understand war.

Returning to the barge ahead of the other guests and finding herself alone with Dan, Maddie let curiosity get the best of her. "So what's your story?"

"Not much to tell. Small-town boy with dreams of escaping the restraints of country living and seeing the world."

"I can understand that." She leaned against a row of seats. "The town in West Texas where I grew up was split into two categories. Kin and folks who were almost kin."

Dan laughed. "Sounds like the same town I grew up in. Except I was raised in rural Kentucky. Do you still live in Texas?"

"No. Didn't have any interest in seeing the world but the ocean always appealed to me. Florida seemed to be better suited to retirees, so I wound up at UCLA."

Standing beside her, arms crossed, he looked incredibly handsome in his uniform. "Lots of beautiful country on the West Coast."

"I love just sitting on the beach and doing nothing but listening to the waves roll in. When I visit my parents, I could spend all day and night by the ocean."

He nodded. "Water can be very healing."

"Is that why you picked the navy?" She noticed the chunky admiral and his gray-haired wife boarding the barge, and wished for a few more minutes alone with Dan. The tour was coming to an end. The *Arizona* was the last portion, and soon she and her folks would return to the airport, and she'd know little more about this man than she had when she had first plowed into him at LAX.

Almost as if reading her mind, Dan's gaze flickered from hers to the approaching couple, and he took hold of her elbow. "Let's step outside." Ducking left behind a support pillar, he led the way around to the sliver of a rear deck and, facing away from the admiral, leaned forward, his forearms resting on the rail. "You were saying?"

"I was asking if the healing power of water is why you joined the navy."

He shook his head. "I got a full-ride football scholarship to Tennessee State. Near the end of the first season I went left, and my knee went right."

Maddie blinked, grimacing slightly at the sympathy pain that shot up her leg.

"It wasn't that bad." He smiled at her. "Doctors said I'd be good to go for next season, but I knew too many guys on the other team would be aiming to take me and my knee out. And even though the NFL wasn't going to happen for me no matter what, if I didn't want my knee to creak every time it rained for the rest of my life, I needed a new plan."

"Ah. A pragmatist."

"I like to think so. I scrambled to find ways to make enough money to stay in college without the football."

"Junior College?"

"No, I didn't want to go back home. I liked Nashville. It may not be *big city* to most people, but it was enough for me to know I never wanted to go back to living in the backwoods of anywhere again. I tried a few things but figured out quickly that I needed something more substantial. ROTC fit the bill."

"Sir, ma'am." One of the boat operators leaned through the opening. "If you'd please step inside. We're ready to pull out."

"Of course," she and Dan replied in unison. For some reason that made her smile. *He* made her smile.

Back inside with the other passengers, they took a seat beside her parents. "I cannot thank you enough," her mom said placing her hand on Dan's.

For just a moment Maddie saw a flicker of surprise in his eyes before he bobbed his head, and everyone's attention shifted to the monument shrinking in their wake.

Her dad looked at his wrist. "We probably still have an hour or so to take in a few sights."

"Yes." Yvette nodded. "I was chatting earlier with one of the officers stationed here, and he said finding a cab to get back to town wouldn't be any problem."

"What did you have in mind?" Dan asked.

Yvette pointed a thumb at her husband. "Mr. Retro TV here wants to do a Hawaii Five-O tour."

Dan turned to look at Maddie, and she could see the question in his eyes. "The opening shots from the TV show. Dad wants to see the punchbowl, Iolani Palace, Diamond Head—"

"And the girl stepping out of the ocean. Don't forget that one," Randy said with a face-splitting grin.

Dan burst out laughing. "I'm sure that won't be a problem. I have a rental car. With GPS. If you wouldn't mind my company a little longer, I'd be glad to play chauffeur."

Was it wrong for Maddie's heart to do a little jig? All she'd get was an extra hour with soon-to-be former US Navy Captain Daniel O'Neil. But at the moment she couldn't think of anything she wanted more.

"School pictures were the next day." Yvette wiped the tears

still slipping down her cheek and then let out another chuckle. "And my sweet little four-year-old girl"—she swiped at her eyes again and sputtered a muffled laugh—"had a reverse mohawk."

Dan found himself swallowing a chuckle. From the moment they'd left the harbor, Randy and Yvette had been sharing stories of their little girl's childhood, and Madeleine—or Maddie as her family called her—rolled her eyes and laughed with them. Ignoring his schedule for the remainder of the afternoon and *winging it* with the Harpers was proving to be an outstanding decision.

"For the rest of the school year she wore a comb-over like a balding banker." Yvette laughed out loud again.

"Don't let her laughter fool you. She was spitting mad when she found Madeleine sitting in front of the mirror cutting away at her hair," Randy added.

"I merely wanted to trim my bangs."

"Trim?" Yvette repeated.

Maddie offered a coy smile, and Dan had to admit the woman had a great disposition. Her parents had told story after story, and Maddie had laughed at herself with ease, only occasionally pretending playfully to pout. "I didn't like them anymore."

Yvette shook her head. Randy winked at Maddie, and Dan felt the pang of regret for having missed out all these years on a relationship with his own daughter.

Turning the corner, Dan pulled into the circular drive in front of the famed statue of Lady Columbia on the far wall of the National Cemetery of the Pacific.

"So many years of watching Steve McGarrett and Book-'Em Danno and I never realized this was a cemetery." Randy's gaze lingered on the horizon.

Because of the time constraints Dan let Randy and Yvette out at the foot of the wall, and circled the U-shaped drive allowing them to take a few photos and walk around. "You have a great relationship with your parents."

"I like to think so." Maddie had taken the front seat, and, undoing her seat belt, she shifted sideways to face him. "Sometimes I'm so glad they live several states away, and then sometimes I so wish they didn't live several states away. What about you? Have a good relationship with your parents?"

"I like to think so," he mimicked. "Mom fusses over me, making all my favorite foods when I come home, which isn't often enough. Dad used to work at the local factory when we were growing up. Now he likes to build things. We spend most of the time holed up in his workshop. Last time I was there, we made a rocking chair for my grandmother."

"Really?" She leaned forward a bit. "How wonderful to be able to share that. I wish I could do something so lasting."

"Build a rocker?"

"Create a family heirloom. Mom's handy with knitting and crocheting. The gene must have skipped a generation because I've got two left thumbs. Do you have any siblings?"

"Oh, yeah. I'm number five of eight." Going to college and having his own bed with only one roommate had seemed like living high on the hog to him. After graduation, when he started through the EOD training pipeline, sharing a bathroom with a bunch of guys felt just like home.

Maddie leaned back as he pulled up to the curb. "I can't imagine that many brothers and sisters. I could have killed Nick more than once, and he was all I had."

He parked the car for Randy and Yvette to climb in. "But the important thing is you didn't."

"Didn't what, dear?" Yvette asked as she settled into the backseat.

"Kill Nick."

"Of course not. You don't look good in prison stripes." The two women grinned as if they knew something no one else did and then burst out laughing.

Next was a drive through downtown past Iolani Palace.

"It says here"—Randy lifted his nose from one of the brochures—"that the palace replaced gas lights with electric five years before the White House."

Stopped at a red light, Dan pointed to the familiar

structure known to fans of the long running 1960s TV show as five-O headquarters. "At the time the original show was filmed this was the government building. Not long after the show first aired, the state offices moved out and renovations began. The palace has been a museum since the late seventies."

"How do you know all that?" Maddie asked.

He shrugged. "You learn all sorts of odd television trivia when stationed in Hawaii. On the way to the airport, I'll drive by the marina that was used for the opening scene of Gilligan's Island."

Maddie and her mom sang in chorus, "A three-hour tour," and Randy chimed in for the remainder of the iconic television theme song.

From there they drove past the statue of King Kamehameha, the Aloha Tower, the Ilikai Hotel where McGarrett had stood on the rooftop, and Diamond Head, stopping to take the occasional photo. With a little time to spare before they would need to leave for the airport, the group parked at one of the beachfront hotels and strolled out to watch the sunset.

"You were right." Maddie let her fingertips barely fall against his arm.

Needing more effort than he would have expected, he pried his tongue off the roof of his mouth. "About what?"

Without a word she raised her other arm and pointed to the shore. Sure enough, out of the water, just like the opening credits, a bikini-clad brunette rose from the surf. Shaking off the water, she made her way onto the beach, and Dan thought, as beautiful a vision as the native woman made, she didn't compare to the lady standing beside him. Fair alabaster-toned skin proclaimed that, despite her love of the ocean, Madeleine didn't spend much time in the sun. Her warm smile put strangers at ease. Long brown hair covered her shoulders and drew a man's eye to her feminine frame. But big brown eyes that held laughter and brimmed with love for her family was what had him by the throat and wouldn't let go. For a short minute he indulged in considering just how inappropriate it would be to start a relationship with a much younger woman.

Only right away he realized more than just an age difference was against them as long-distance dating never worked out. He'd tried a few times when he was younger to do the will-you-wait-for-me relationships. Learning that lesson, he'd instead put his energies into his naval career. Some of the men he'd known in EOD had gotten lucky; they had both their work and had met the kind of woman who could stick through hell or high water. He hadn't been one of the lucky ones. But then again, in a couple more months, he would neither belong to Uncle Sam nor have to deal with hell *or* high water.

CHAPTER FIVE

"\"**M**aybe you should cut back a little more on your workload?" His wife's feet on his lap, Billy Everrett switched back and forth, rubbing one foot then the other.

Hands resting loosely on her rounded tummy, Angela looked to her husband with only one eye open. "Who do you suggest I throw to the wolves?"

"I don't understand why you consider your colleagues *wolves*."

She blew out a sigh. "I don't. Most of the agents in my office are more than capable to buy or sell a house. It's the other stuff that is hard to pass off."

By *other stuff* his wife was no doubt referring to the hours she spent doing rough sketches of room renovations for her clients to use when interviewing contractors. Or the afternoons spent accompanying a buyer shopping for furniture to decorate the newly purchased home. Or poring over color samples and swatches for one of her investors. "You really do too much."

"I know. I keep saying I'm going to charge for all the extras but—"

"You love it," he finished for her.

"Yeah. I really do. And every once in a while I get to help people with more than just buying or decorating a home."

"You're talking about that young woman who needed an investigator?"

Angela squinted at him with one eye again and nodded.

"Was Brooklyn able to help her find who she was looking for?"

Angela bobbed her head and let her eyes fall shut. "Yeah. I think it's been at least a few months now. I have to admit, Brooklyn is amazing."

"He is."

"And that associate of his is a real hoot."

Billy had to think about that a minute before he remembered about Brooklyn's grandmother-in-law's ex-cop husband. Though, from the stories Billy had heard over time, he suspected the grandmother was the true firecracker in that family.

"Do you think they'll ever come to visit? I'd love to meet him and Sharla in person."

"Hard to say. Their baby is due before ours."

"Then maybe we should go there?"

"You mean now?" Billy's hand stilled. "Before the baby?"

"No, I'd hate to miss the birth of Nick and Kara's baby."

"You want to practice on Baby Harper?" Billy ran his fingers up the back of Angela's calf, kneading at a particularly stubborn knot.

"I've been practicing for motherhood my whole life. It's Kara who might need some help when that baby arrives. There was no Diaper Changing 101 in law school. Once her aunt and Nick's mom are gone, she'll probably need me."

Even Billy knew his wife was absolutely correct. Kara was a fantastic litigator. Wonderful mother to Nick's son, Bradley. But so far she seemed a bit overwhelmed by the whole preparing-for-baby concept. "So we've established we're not traveling because Kara may need you. And you're not ready to hand off any of your current clients—"

"There are only two of them left."

"I thought you were working with four people?"

She shook her head. "Even though I thought the probate court was never going to sign off on the contract for Carolyn Porter's house, we finally closed last week. And Mr. Sobel decided he wanted to wait a few more months to list his house."

Billy bit his lip and refrained from commenting. It was

people like the Sobels who made his wife's job so much harder, working until all hours only to have the clients back off and then return in a few months and have her start all over again.

"Oh." Both of Angela's eyes popped open. "I forgot to mention that I've invited a few people to your mom's barbecue."

"I'm sure that will be fine. We all know she's going to invite half the town herself."

"I know, and most of these clients have moved here from somewhere else. One of your mom's parties is a great way for them to settle in. And maybe even make a few new friends."

"As long as making these new friends doesn't wear you and Junior out."

"Junior and I are just fine. Besides, with your fingers, as long as you keep rubbing my feet like that, I could probably face demons and devils on my own—and win."

"Yeah, well, here's hoping we don't ever get to test that theory. Oh, by the way, Nick called to say his mother's flight is coming in late. Do you still want to do dinner with them?"

"How late is *late*?"

"Almost nine."

"Nope." She shook her head. "Junior is demanding I eat pretty soon. We'll never make it until nine. Maddie and I can talk shop another day."

"Are you still scheming for Nick's sister to move to Kona?"

"You bet. I also want to introduce her to a few people, get her feeling like this could be home."

Billy's chest rumbled with laughter. "I never thought I'd hear myself say this, but you remind me of my mother."

Angela flashed a cheesy grin. "I'll take that as a compliment."

"It is." He loved his mother. She had a multitude of admirable qualities and was loved by everyone. But she also happened to be the biggest busybody he'd ever met and was determined to marry off every single person of legal age.

"All we have to do for the next month is keep my mother and her matchmaking schemes away from Madeleine."

Angela sputtered with laughter. "Could we try to stop Mauna Loa from erupting instead? Your mother is a true force of nature."

That she was. He just hoped Madeleine Harper wasn't anywhere on his mother's matchmaking radar.

While Randy and Yvette walked into the hotel in search of a cool drink, Dan sat on the beach beside Maddie, wondering why he felt so comfortable with a woman he'd only known a few hours. "Your parents are quite a couple."

"Sometimes I wonder if I've gone to sleep and woken up in a Norman Rockwell painting."

"So they're like this all the time. Not just on vacation?"

"Well, it's been a while since I've lived with them, but I think it's safe to say, yes. They're like this all the time."

"That's great."

Maddie blew out a wistful sigh. "Yeah. It really is. Most of the time I doubt I'll ever meet anyone who I'll connect with like that."

"You will."

"I don't know. I'm starting to think my father is a mutation. He must have a Z chromosome that, unlike the regular Y chromosome, doesn't have the idiot gene."

"Ouch."

"Sorry. It's been a rough few months on the dating front. But I am holding out hope for a few good men to outgrow the inferior gene. Nick seems to have."

"That would be the idiot gene?"

Maddie held back a laugh. "Yeah. Nick is not only turning out to be a pretty good husband, he and his wife have a similar thing going like Mom and Dad. They're really cute together too. I expect it won't be too long before they can read each other's minds as well."

"It is a bit uncanny how your parents do that. I noticed,

a few times, all it took was one look, and then one or the other spoke for both of them. Once in a while you get an XO—I mean, second in command—who can almost read your mind, but nothing like that." He had also had a few teammates who had worked with him like his own shadow, but he didn't want to go down that path now. Her parents would be back soon, and he just wanted to enjoy Maddie's company for the little time they had left. "Your mom is also pretty stoked about the grandkids."

"Oh, yes."

"Especially the new baby."

"It's not that she isn't excited to see Bradley, but this is her first grand*baby*."

"Your brother was stationed overseas when Bradley was born?"

"My brother didn't know when his son was born. Or, more accurately, he didn't know he even had a son. He didn't discover then-five-year-old Bradley's existence until the mother was diagnosed with cancer."

"Oh."

"It was quite a shock to everyone, but Mom was over the moon from the start. She dotes on that kid like he was the Second Coming. And I know the new baby is going to be even worse."

"I'm sure." He certainly could relate to the shock of discovering having a child. Though finding out that he had an adult daughter wasn't quite the same thing, it was a shock nonetheless.

"They tell me Mom almost passed out from the news. But she recovered quickly. Nick had one heck of a learning curve too, but, fortunately for him, his wife has pretty good instincts. Though she wasn't married to him yet at the time."

"It must have been hard for him."

"Once he got over the surprise of it all, he had to deal with the anger. It was difficult for him to believe that someone he'd loved enough to want to marry and raise a family with would have kept such a secret from him. No matter how many children he and Kara have, he'll never get back those early years he missed with Bradley."

"No." Dan leaned his forearms across the tops of his knees. "No, he can't."

His mind circled back to that day months ago when his doorbell rang. Living in a quiet little place just outside base, he'd been enjoying a relaxing afternoon watching the Titan's game. He couldn't imagine who would be ringing his bell instead of sitting in front of the TV watching the last minutes of the 21–24 game.

On the other side of the open door stood a lovely young blonde, nibbling on her lower lip. "Hello."

This was not the time to be selling magazine subscriptions. "Hello."

"My name is Carolyn, and I was hoping you might have a few minutes to talk."

He glanced over her shoulder, wondering if some thug or other criminal with an agenda was lurking in the hallway to his apartment, then switched his attention to the TV screen. "This isn't the best—"

"It's rather important. I've come all the way from Hawaii."

That got his attention. Who the heck comes from Hawaii to sell magazine subscriptions? Once again he looked at the TV and figured, if she wasn't a well-disguised mass murder about to shoot him dead and rob him blind, he could always replay the final minutes of the game later. "Sure, come on in."

The young lady had a grip on the strap of her purse that turned her knuckles white. For her, whatever was up was very serious.

"I'm not sure where to start."

"The beginning is usually a good place." He considered offering her something to drink but decided to wait until he knew what this was all about.

"I graduated in May from the University of Hawaii and took a job in Kona. I'm an accountant." She paused as though expecting him to comment. When he said nothing, she continued. "My mom really wanted me to go to law school and someday join her practice."

"Some parents are really into family businesses." His dad had hoped none of his kids would follow in his footsteps to the assembly line.

"Mom worked hard to get her degree and to build her practice. While most of her friends were going out and partying, she put herself through law school. Her career was her entire focus. Then one day she looked up and realized she was thirty-five years old and had no one to share her success with."

He certainly understood that. At forty-one he had a lot of nieces and nephews but no real home of his own, something he was trying not to think about as he approached his twenty years in the navy and early retirement.

"Anyhow a couple of years later she decided it was do or die, and she had artificial insemination."

Uh-oh. Dan started doing some fast math. Recent graduate made her twenty-one, maybe twenty-two. And twenty-two years ago he'd been a stupid freshman looking for an easy way to make some fast cash when one of his teammates mentioned donating sperm. But if this young lady had taken time off before starting college, then the math wouldn't work. "How old are you?"

"Twenty-one."

The math worked. This could all be coincidence, but he was pretty sure he knew why she was here. But how?

"I've wondered my whole life about my father. My mother had some basic facts she got from the sperm bank. Height, weight, education. A basic medical history. Even a photograph. But not much more."

Dan blinked. It was a reflexive action like breathing. Speaking wasn't an option.

"Mom and I had made plans from an early age for me to save and position myself so I could buy a small condo after college instead of renting. I've got this fabulous Realtor in Kona. Absolutely the best. Mom only met her once, but she just loves her. And Mom's not easy to win over either. They got along like a house on fire."

He nodded this time. Maybe this was going somewhere

different than he first thought.

"My Realtor's husband has an old navy buddy who used to be a SEAL and now he owns a private security company. He's a top-notch private investigator."

Dan found himself studying her face, looking for commonalities.

"I'd been trying to get files released since I'd turned eighteen. The donor didn't sign an identification option."

He remembered that. Donors could authorize contact by the offspring once they reached the legal age of consent. Only eighteen himself at the time, he hadn't seen the point.

"But Luke is amazing. In only a few days he gave me a name and address." She pulled a small legal-size envelope from her purse, emptied the contents and handed Dan the pages. "Yours."

CHAPTER SIX

Dan stood by the trunk of his rental car at the Honolulu airport and unloaded the two carry-on bags for Maddie and her parents. "It's been a pleasure."

"Now don't forget," Randy said, "first vacation you get, come on down to Port Aransas, and we'll get in some serious fishing."

"Will do." There had been an exchange of email addresses, which most likely would never be used.

Yvette grinned at him. "Knock 'em dead at the symposium." For a split second he thought she was reaching forward to hug him only to have her back up instead.

Madeleine yanked on the handle for the carry-on and, straightening her shoulders, offered a tired smile. No surprise considering evening in Honolulu was late night on the mainland, but nonetheless he thought he detected a hint of sadness playing peekaboo with exhaustion. She waved a thumb at her mother. "What she said." Then she stuck that same hand out to him.

"Thank you." Glad for the slightest excuse to touch, he folded his hand around hers. Their handshake lasted only as long as socially acceptable, even though he wanted very much to pull her into a hug for a proper good-bye. "Congratulations again on the new baby."

He'd said it before but felt the need to say it one more time. He was oddly pleased that this time Madeleine and her parents would be involved in her niece's or nephew's life from the beginning. And not for the first time today he felt a physical ache in his chest at the years he'd lost with his daughter. *Daughter.* The word alone seemed as foreign as the concept. Carolyn was still a stranger. A polite stranger. With his DNA.

The happy family walked away, and he resisted the urge to linger until they were out of sight. He'd also resisted the urge to meet up with them while he was in Kona. His reason for coming this far was to get to know Carolyn better. To start working on that father-daughter relationship that meant so much to her. Not that she'd come right out and said so. But he hadn't moved up through the ranks to captain in only twenty years without being able to read between the lines and behind facades. And after today he was more than ready to do something about that family he'd never taken the time to have.

Madeleine followed her parents out the door of the aircraft and down the stairs to the tarmac. She loved the old-fashioned Kona airport. Honolulu had been nice, especially the company, but Kona felt like she'd finally landed in Hawaii. The only thing missing was for her friends and family to greet her in grass skirts with floral leis.

From the bottom of the stairs she could see her parents ahead, already scooping Bradley into their arms. Hugs and kisses abounded. Maddie hefted her purse over her shoulder and shifted the carry-on to her other hand, unable to shake an odd sense of restlessness that had nagged her ever since Dan had left her at the Honolulu airport. Everything about spending the afternoon together had been different than an ordinary afternoon of tourism. Leaving him behind felt like leaving an old friend. Struggling with the unexpected sense of loss had made the one-hour flight to Kona seem longer than a round-the-world trip.

And then she thought for the gazillionth time about the short time she and Dan had spent together. Though he hadn't given her many details, she got the impression from the little he'd said about his daughter that he hadn't been a big part of her life growing up. A fate that affected a good number of military men. Especially during wartime when deployments away from home could go on forever. And something that he seemed determined to make up for. In the short time Maddie had had with Dan, she had more of a feeling about him than any actual information. She didn't even know what he was doing now that he'd retired from the navy. Nor where he would call home. Though she did find out he'd be spending a week, maybe longer if needed, with his daughter helping her set up her new house. And Maddie got the distinct impression he wished he could do more.

Which of course left her thinking about her own relationships. Though she loved living in Southern California, no matter how many friends she made, no matter how close they became, none of them would ever be the same as family. Through no fault of her own she'd missed her nephew's early years, and, now, if she stayed in San Diego, she would miss the better part of the baby's life as well. Yes, she'd arrange to visit as she'd done a couple of times for Bradley, but her career didn't allow for much vacation time, and, even so, a few weeks a year wouldn't be the same as day-to-day involvement in a child's early life. She may not be his mother or even his grandmother, but that didn't mean she loved the kid any less.

As soon as she'd made it to the covered gate area, Bradley's small voice squealed, "Aunt Maddie!" Squirming out of his grandmother's hold, her young nephew shot into her arms.

"How's my favorite young man?" Letting go of her bags, she wrapped her arms around him, hefting him up and twirling him about. "I missed you!" It was hard to believe how much she'd come to love this little squirt in less than a year and a half. It didn't hurt that the kid was both adorable and smart as a whip.

"Daddy says you're going to be here for a whole month."

"That's right." She hadn't said anything to her brother yet about considering moving to Hawaii. For more than a few months she'd been teetering between moving and staying put. Her job or her family. Today the scales dipped farther to one side.

"My room is all ready for you. I helped Moms make the bed with new flower sheets. Dad says we have to help her until the new baby comes."

Maddie's gaze flew up to her brother. Nick bobbed his head. His expression warm, yet sad. "You're such a good gentleman," Maddie said to Bradley.

"Dad says that too. He says that's what Mommy wanted for me."

This time Nick smiled down at his son. His eyes filled with pride.

"And you did a wonderful job too." Kara held out her hand, and Bradley eagerly took his stepmother's hand.

Maddie and her mom let Kara and Bradley get slightly ahead of them, then Yvette looked at her son. "This is something new."

Nick smiled. "Yeah. He started calling Kara *Moms* a few weeks ago. Never *Mom* or *Mommy*. Always *Moms*. And whenever he mentions Patty Ann, it's always *Mommy*."

"So my grandson figured out a way to have a new mother in his life without giving up the first one." Yvette smiled broadly. "Seriously smart kid. Takes after his grandmother."

Maddie linked arms with her brother and walked behind their mother, laughing. "It's nice to be all together again, isn't it?"

"Can't think of much better."

"Had Mom mentioned to you yet that she and Dad are thinking about moving out here? Permanently."

Nick's gait slowed. "Seriously?"

"Yep." Maddie nodded. Stopping at the baggage area, she leaned in closer. "I wasn't going to say anything to you until I spoke with Billy's wife, but I've been doing a lot of thinking today about lost opportunities, and, well, I think it might be time for me to have a little change of scenery also."

"How much of a change?"

"Kona."

Nick's brows arched high on his forehead. "For real?"

The buzzer sounded; the carousel began to move, and Maddie grinned at her brother's surprise. "For real."

A wide smile took over his face. "I'm going to hold you to that."

Yvette pointed to the first bag coming around the carousel. "That's mine."

Nick pulled it aside just as his mother pointed to the next bag. And the next. When another came along and she pointed to it as well, Nick set it with the others, asking, "How many suitcases did you bring?"

"A good grandmother can't arrive empty-handed."

"Maybe so, but Mom you've got enough luggage here to last through winter in Alaska. Good thing we brought two cars or I'd be strapping you and Dad to the roof."

"Nonsense." Yvette lightly smacked her son's arm. "Dad would drive. You would have walked." Turning to face Kara and her daughter, Yvette rubbed her hands together enthusiastically. "So, do we have a baby pool going?"

Nick nodded. "Absolutely. Jonathan's keeping it at the shop. Let him know what you want, and he'll pencil you in."

"Anyone take Valentine's Day yet?" Randy asked.

"Not yet." Nick shook his head and swallowed a chuckle. "But you may be on to something. Billy's mom seems to think the baby is in a hurry. As a matter of fact, we're all invited over for a barbecue this weekend before the baby comes."

Yvette's brows knit together. "Does she know something we should?"

"Nope. Kara's doctor is expecting her to go past her due date. He calls it first-baby-take-your-time syndrome."

Randy shook his head. "I'm sure my grandchild won't give you any trouble. But just in case, I've got ten bucks on Valentine's Day."

CHAPTER SEVEN

"How's this?" Dan slid the large framed photo of the original Grand Ole Opry house onto the hook he'd just nailed into the wall and stepped back.

"I love it!" Carolyn squealed. She'd squealed after each and every picture he'd hung for her this morning. Whether she was normally this jubilant or was just still riding her new-house high, he wasn't sure. But he had to admit he was tempted to squeal with her.

"What's next on the list?" In the two days since he'd arrived in Kona, he had installed roll-out shelves in the kitchen, added shelves to the linen closet, and reconfigured the shelves in the pantry. He would have gladly continued adding, cutting and installing anything his daughter wanted, but he had to admit he'd been very glad when the next thing on the list had only involved a hammer and a level.

"We've done all the heavy pieces. I can hang the smaller ones later."

"Or we can do it all now and get it done." He might technically be retired from the military, but he still had a sense of order that was hard to let go of. And not finishing a job when all the equipment was out and ready to be used, even if only a hammer and a box of nails, seemed like an egregious misuse of time. Besides, he loved how Carolyn's face lit up every time he offered to do something for her.

No wonder daughters around the world had their fathers wrapped around their fingers. He couldn't even begin to fathom the hardships he would have endured to make his little girl happy—had he known he had one.

The last room to be tackled with the remaining framed

pictures was the guest room. He'd hung a gorgeous array of ocean photographs. His favorite had been taken around sunrise. The way the lights glimmered off the sand and the beaches was stunning. "This one is truly breathtaking."

"Thank you."

"You have a magnificent eye. I'm having a hard time reconciling a by-the-numbers accountant with the person who took these."

"Everyone needs a hobby."

"Yes, but not everyone's hobbies require talent. I like hiking and rock climbing."

"Maybe next time you go, I'll come with you."

"You like to climb?"

She laughed. "No, but I'd like to take pictures of you climbing."

"Not so sure even you could make those worth looking at." He gathered up the level he'd used for the larger frames that required two nails, along with the box of nails and pencil. "Where shall I put these?"

"Until I get a shed, I've been putting all the tools we've bought in this closet." She tugged at the bifold doors. They didn't budge, and she pulled a little harder. The knob came off in her hand, throwing her off balance and shoving her into him.

For a split second his mind wandered back to when he had first met Maddie before he shook his thoughts clear. After retrieving the knob, he examined the top and bottom of the sticky doors. "Looks like something else on the list to fix."

"We might have to deal with the rest of the list later. It's almost time to leave for the party."

"I still think you should go on without me. This would be a good time for your old man to head back to the hotel and take a nap." Not that he had any intention of actually napping.

Carolyn rolled her eyes and blew out a sigh. "Really? You're not that old."

Holding back a smile, Dan shrugged a casual shoulder. Since discovering he had an adult daughter, he found himself feeling downright ancient. What he really wanted to do about now was put on his running shoes and take a long jog by the shore. Since coming to Hawaii, he'd had way too much food for thought. First he was having a hard time getting Madeleine Harper out of his mind. Which meant he really did need to think about adding a good woman to his new life plans. Just one more suited to becoming a grandmother someday soon and not a first-time mother.

And then Carolyn. She'd offered her guest room when they'd discussed his coming out after the symposium, but he'd not been comfortable with that so he'd booked a hotel room. DNA or not, except for the day she'd come to his apartment to find him, and a handful of telephone conversations since, they were still pretty much strangers. Which was the rest of what he had to think about. In only two days he could feel the relationship shifting. Carolyn wasn't quite as careful around him. The eye roll a little while ago was something she wouldn't have done when he'd first arrived. And snippets of a biting sense of humor were beginning to appear.

Though he was sure she had a great deal of her mother in her, the more time he spent with Carolyn, the more he saw of his own family. When she laughed really hard, her nose crinkled just like his mother's. In the heat of the afternoon the day before she'd grabbed her hair and did one of those twisty things leaving a pile on top of her head and showing off a profile just like his sister Tammy. But the way she teased him at dinner last night about how he ate his spaghetti, he would have sworn she'd grown up right beside him and his brother Matt. Absolutely amazing how two people who had never lived together could be so alike.

And no doubt, if he spent more time with her, he'd discover even more family traits. Which is what he had to think about. He had twenty-two years to make up for, and that was going to be very hard to do three thousand miles away via telephone with once- or twice-a-year visits.

"Hello?" Carolyn waved her hand in front of his face. "Maybe you're right, and you are suffering from early onset dementia. I may have to call the nursing home now. Reserve you a room." A broad cheeky grin and exceptionally wide innocent eyes screamed the O'Neil sense of humor. Yep, if the DNA tests hadn't confirmed her PI's report, the last two days certainly did.

"Oh, lord, it smells good in here." Maddie lifted her nose in the air and took a deep whiff. She loved the smell of fresh-baked anything.

Holding a mixing bowl in front of her, her mother scooped the dark orange mixture into a pan. "I told Maile I'd make a few of my sweet potato pies for this afternoon."

"Oh, heavens, what's that?" Hands on her lower back, Kara came waddling in the kitchen behind Maddie, taking in the wonderful aroma of baking pies.

"Mom's making her famous sweet potato pies."

"That explains it. The last time you made pie, I didn't get home until long after that delectable aroma was gone." Kara put her hand on her tummy and laughed. "Ooh, Junior smells it too. It's unanimous. You can bake pies for us anytime."

"That's what I've been thinking," Yvette said.

Maddie and Kara glanced at each other quickly before looking back to her mother.

"Randy and I have talked this through one more time, and we've come to a decision. When we go home after this trip, we're going to get the condo in Port Aransas ready to go on the market. Hopefully by late spring. As soon as it sells, we're moving to Kona."

Kara did her best in her very pregnant condition to fling herself at her mother-in-law. "That's fabulous news."

Sniffing at the air like a bloodhound, Nick followed the scent to the oven. "What's fabulous news?"

Yvette set the bowl on the island and, picking up the pie pan, moved to her son's side, nudging him with her elbow. "Your father and I have decided to move to Hawaii."

Grinning, Nick opened the oven door for her. "How

soon are you coming? Or is the container with all your worldly possessions on the way already?"

Yvette slid the pan onto the rack and, grabbing the oven mitts, brought out the cooked pie to set on the cooling rack. "Comedian. Though we've been thinking about it for a while, we only last night made up our minds."

"There isn't that much for you to do. The place is in great shape, and you shouldn't have any trouble selling," Maddie added. "The Texas market is really hot. Even for vacation homes."

"I was hoping you'd say that. Daddy and I don't want to wait too long, but we don't want the expense of running two households either."

"A wise choice." Kara eased onto a kitchen chair.

"You okay, honey?" Yvette studied her daughter-in-law.

"I'm fine. Just once I wouldn't mind if this baby slept at night like I do."

Maddie took in the room. Her brother and mother looked like matching bookends, both frowning at Kara as though she'd announced she'd be giving birth to an alien. "How about some tea?"

"Good idea." Kara put her hands on the table and pushed up.

"No," three voices chorused, with Yvette gesturing to her children to give her the floor. "I'll get you a cup."

"Anyone want some juice?" Maddie asked from the fridge.

"No thanks," all the voices echoed.

"Oh, I forgot to tell you." She poured herself a cup and turned to her brother. "Margaret Alani is coming by to pick up Bradley. He's in his room changing. She's taking him and her grandson over to Maile's early."

"I'd better go check on him." Nick turned to leave the room, paused to kiss his wife on the cheek and continued on his way.

Yvette set a warm cup of caffeine-free tea in front of Kara, and, before Maddie could take her seat, the doorbell rang. "I'll get it."

Margaret Alani was best friends with Billy Everrett's mother, Maile, the woman throwing this afternoon's welcome soiree. "Madeleine, dear. So nice to see you."

"You too! Come on in."

Margaret's grandson made a beeline for Bradley's room, and she smiled after the little boy with so much love it strengthened Maddie's resolve to move closer to her own family.

"Just for a minute. I promised Maile I'd be there to help her."

"If Maile needs more help, we'd be happy to go over early too." Maddie closed the door behind their guest. "Mom loves to fuss over parties."

"Not necessary. We're just getting all our ducks in a row. Plenty of nice single people coming. It should be lots of fun."

Alarm bells probably should have sounded at the use of "single people," but, since Maddie was only a visitor, her matchmaker radar was taking a break.

"Anyone special?" Nick ushered the boys into the living room.

"That nice Dr. Shepherd said he'd come. And there's a new lawyer at Brian Simm's law firm. And—"

"Can we go now?" her grandson interrupted.

"Oh, yes. Yes, let's go." Margaret turned to Maddie. "You look pretty as a picture in that dress. You'll be the belle of the ball." Without waiting for a response, Margaret turned and hurried out the door with the two boys rushing ahead of her.

And with that, Maddie's matchmaker radar sprang to life. "Did I miss something?"

Nick placed a reassuring hand on his sister's shoulder. "Nope. My advice is to steer clear of Billy's mother and her friend, and, if you're really lucky, they won't even notice you're there."

"Fat chance. But," Kara added, "on the bright side, they've never successfully matched up anyone, so you probably have nothing to worry about."

Probably?

"Meeting a nice man wouldn't be such a bad thing." Her mother began mixing the last batch of pie fillings.

No, it wouldn't be such a bad thing. Except there had been only one nice man on her mind for the last four days, and the odds of Maile Everrett springing him on her were no better than her springing over anything without falling on her rear first. Unless, of course, a handsome former navy sailor were nearby to catch her.

CHAPTER EIGHT

To Dan the little barbecue at a friend's house looked more like a banquet for visiting dignitaries. He was pretty sure he hadn't seen this much food at one time outside of a mess hall. Of course the mess hall food couldn't compare to what he'd already sampled.

"What do you think this is?" he asked Carolyn.

"Not sure." She took a bite. "Oh, my. I think it's a coconut fritter."

He bit into the small lumpy blob. Oh, yeah. Definitely never ate anything like this in the mess halls.

"I'm so sorry I'm late." An attractive brunette with an obvious baby bump hurried over to Carolyn's side.

"No, no big deal. I brought my father. He and I have been sampling the hors d'oeuvres. These are wonderful."

"Maile Everrett is probably hands-down the best cook on the island. Which is probably why everyone who's invited to one of her parties always comes." Angela stuck out her hand. "I'm Angela Everrett. I sold your daughter her house."

"Dan O'Neil. She's told me a lot about you. You did good."

"Thanks." Angela smiled. "But don't believe a word she says."

"Too late, I already do."

Before Angela could form a rebuttal, the hostess, a rotund native woman in a bright floral outfit, hurried across the patio in his and Carolyn's direction. "Carolyn, dear." The effervescent woman extended her hand and rather than wait for Carolyn to accept, somehow maneuvered Carolyn out from behind the table. "I have someone I'd like for you to meet."

Wide-eyed Carolyn looked to Angela, who merely smiled and shrugged.

"You needn't worry," Angela said matter-of-factly to him.

Dan hadn't realized he'd been frowning until the young Realtor addressed him. His gaze had followed the pair as the older woman led his daughter into a small huddle of men.

"My mother-in-law is pretty harmless." She sipped what Dan assumed by the drink's light color to be ginger ale. "From what I understand, she and my late father-in-law had a very happy marriage, and, now that he's gone, she seems determined to find the same wedded bliss for everyone on the island."

"Including my daughter?"

Angela chuckled. "Most likely."

"But she's only twenty-two." He felt the furrow between his brows deepen. Even to his own ears that sounded way too much like whining. Or worse, a father unwilling to accept his baby girl had grown up. Except he'd never had a baby girl, only the grown-up version.

"And she's perfectly safe. Maile huffs and fusses a lot, but she's yet to pick the right two people."

The Realtor's pleasant chuckle did little to assuage his concerns as laughter burst from the group of men surrounding his daughter. Lips pressed together, he wondered if announcing how many different ways he knew how to kill a man with his bare hands would douse the new suitors' interest.

"Glad you're here," Angela mumbled to an approaching male.

Still vigilant of his daughter's company, Dan only half listened to what Angela said.

"This is my husband, Billy. Honey, this is Carolyn Porter's father."

"Nice to meet you …" His words trailed off, and the familiar sound of shoe heels knocking together caught Dan's attention in time to see the house of a man throw his shoulders back and snap to attention. "Captain, sir."

"At ease. Here I'm just Dan." He extended his hand, all the while his mind running through the files of men he'd served with. Or taught. It took him rolling back a lot of years, but he placed the face. One of his best students in EOD. "Nice to see you again."

Billy relaxed and smiled. "I read about your promotion in the *Navy Times*. Congratulations."

"Did you read about my retirement too?"

A wrinkle settled between Billy's brows. "No, sir. I must have missed that."

"Thirty days now. And please don't call me sir. I feel old enough at the moment as it is." His gaze drifted momentarily to his daughter. At least now she was distracted chatting with an attractive redhead. Maybe the Realtor was right, and he was taking this protective-dad thing too seriously. Turning back, he caught a glimpse of the sailor's prosthesis. Sadly not uncommon for men whose careers consisted of disarming things that went boom in the night. "How long have you been out?"

"A few years. I own my dad's dive shop now. Partners with Nick Harper." He put his fingers between his lips and blew a low, sharp and slightly stilted whistle. To the untrained ear it could almost sound like a native bird call.

At least one trained ear recognized the sound for what it was. Another man standing beside a very pregnant woman tapped her arm, whispered in her ear, pointed to the chairs nearby and hurried over to where Dan and Billy stood, shooting his buddy a concerned stare. "What's up?"

Billy cocked his head in Dan's direction. "You're outranked."

The buddy turned to Dan, studying him a moment before his eyes burst round, and he too snapped to attention. Apparently Billy wasn't the only one reading the *Navy Times*.

"At ease."

"Sir, this is a welcome surprise." While both men stood at rest, neither had gone fully to *at ease*.

"Thank you."

"He's with Carolyn. The young woman I sold the little

house over on Kuana Street to."

Two heads gave a curt nod, and Dan saw the glimmer of recognition in their eyes. They'd put two and two together and concluded, justly, that their buddy the former SEAL had helped Carolyn locate her unknown father. And found him.

"How are you enjoying your stay on the Big Island?" Angela asked.

"Haven't seen much of it yet. I've mostly been taking care of the to-do list."

Both men laughed, but it was Billy who first commented, "We know how that goes, sir."

Nick bobbed his head in agreement, and Dan concluded these two must have partnered up for a very long time. "You still in, Nick?"

"No, sir. Didn't have it in me to be a career man."

"I doubt that. But seems all is well for you here." Dan let his gaze wander to the pregnant woman now resting in a comfortable chair.

Nick beamed. "That it is, sir."

Gesturing to the beer bottles with his chin, Dan asked, "So how much of that stuff do you two have to drink before you'll remember to call me by my name?"

"Some habits are hard to break." Billy tipped the neck of his beer bottle at Dan.

"So you all know each other?" Angela asked. "How small a world is that?"

"Actually," Dan started, "the coincidence is only that we're all EOD. Like the SEALs, it's a small, rather tight-knit community. We've never actually served together, but I have been their instructor."

"One of the best," Nick added.

"I don't know about that, but, as long as you knew more when you were through than you did when I got you, I did my job." Dan looked over to the still huddled group of young people. "I should probably go rescue my daughter."

"Actually you stay here and keep talking shop. I want to introduce Carolyn to Nick's sister. She's around here somewhere." Angela cast her gaze around the outdoor area, then stopped and smiled. "There she is."

All three of them followed Angela's watchful gaze, finally settling on a young brunette in a floral sundress with legs all the way to her ... *Holy cow.*

"Dr. Shepherd is a very nice man. For a little while there we thought he was going to end up with our Angela, but she and my Billy were meant to be." Maile Everrett set a bowl of guacamole and chips on the small table.

"I'm sure he is." Maddie did her best not to act too interested without being downright rude. Billy's mom was many things, but subtle wasn't one of them. She did, however, have an endearing nature, despite her matchmaking ambitions.

"Now what are you doing there?" Maile leaned over and scratched the ears of the biggest German shepherd Maddie had ever seen. "No one is going to give you a snack. You go on back in the house and keep an eye on the boys."

The black-and-silver-faced dog seemed to huff and bob his head in obedience to his master before trotting off to the open patio door.

"Well, I'll be." Maddie kept her attention on the beloved family pet. Sure enough, halfway in the door he spotted his charges and plopped on the floor within a few feet to survey his flock. "Fascinating."

"He's a wonderful dog. We got him from a rescue organization for large breeds. The trainer thinks he comes from a true German bloodline. He's so incredibly smart."

She certainly wouldn't argue with that. "He's beautiful too."

"Yes." Maile beamed, then turned her attention from Gunny to Maddie. "Now where did Dr. Shepherd go? Did I mention he's a successful psychiatrist?"

"You did, and I'm sure we'll bump into each other before I return to San Diego."

Angela strolled up to her mother-in-law. "Looking for someone?"

"Dr. Shepherd."

Maile missed the roll of her daughter-in-law's eyes, but Maddie caught it and had to cover her mouth with her hand to stifle a laugh.

"Well"—Angela linked arms with Maddie and grinned at her mother-in-law—"if you don't mind, I want to steal Maddie and introduce her to Carolyn. Oh, and we just discovered that Carolyn's father is a former instructor of Nick's and Billy's. If you get a chance, you may want to go say hello. But I'd give it a little while. It sounded to me like they were about to start sharing war stories. You know, the kind about the fish that got away."

Except Maddie knew from years of eavesdropping on her big brother's stories that too many of them weren't even a little exaggerated. She remembered one time in particular from years ago. She'd been lurking in the hall long after everyone's bedtime. Nick and Billy and a few friends from a SEAL team were hanging out. What little she'd heard about saving a woman whose brother had put her in an explosives vest could still give Maddie nightmares. She was often torn between the pride of what her brother had done for a living and the horror that had surrounded it.

Following the direction of Angela's finger, Maddie spotted her brother and Billy laughing and drinking, and then her stomach slid to her feet. The tall, well-built man that Maddie now realized had to be their former instructor was also the same man she'd spent the last few days trying not to think of. If she were a betting woman, she'd lay odds that fate was on her side. Though she'd feel much better about those odds if the object of her attention weren't frowning in her direction.

CHAPTER NINE

Now what? Dan had been staring at Madeleine Harper. Couldn't stop himself from drinking her in. A small part of him wanted to turn cartwheels at the chance to spend some more time with her. The other more sensible part said that this fascination with a woman he'd known for only a few hours was ridiculous. And getting to know her any better would only make walking away more difficult. And he would have to walk away. No way would he put his new relationship with Carolyn at risk by dating someone practically his daughter's age.

He still hadn't looked away when Maddie turned to face him, and their gazes met. It took a few seconds for recognition to set in and shock to take over her face. Finally a shaky smile replaced the surprise, and he forced himself to smile back. And just for good measure, he threw in a nod. But that left him right back to *Now what?*

"Honey, I'd like you to meet Captain O'Neil."

Dan turned his attention back to his former students. Grinning like a cat in a cream factory, Nick had looped an arm around the very pregnant woman Dan had noticed him with earlier.

"How do you do?" She extended her hand. "I'm Kara, also known as Honey, Sweetie and occasionally Sugar. That's when he's feeling his Texas roots."

Dan laughed. "My friends call me Dan."

"That's not how I remember it." Billy took a swallow of his beer.

"That's right," Nick added, still holding onto his wife.

"Another one of those silly call signs?" Kara asked.

"Call signs are for pilots," Nick corrected. "This was

more of a handle."

"Like *Brooklyn*?" she suggested.

"Sort of."

Grinning, Kara turned to Dan. "Is the handle suitable for mixed company?"

He liked this lady. And he was pleased to see Nick married to someone who could keep him on his toes. "Banger, at your services, ma'am. As in *bangers and mash*. For dinner."

"Right." She shook her head, the smile never faltering. "I'll stick with *Dan*."

Noticing the fingers on her right hand gently massaged her tummy, Dan wondered how close she was to delivering, then spotted the four-legged companion who had quietly come and sat at her feet. "I see you have a shadow."

Kara looked down at the canine. "Gunny, I thought Maile told you to watch the boys?"

The big dog made a throaty noise somewhere between a groan and a mumble, nudged her hand with his muzzle, and then, as though debating the immortality of the crab, hesitated before lifting his butt off the floor and turning toward the house again.

"He's been doing that since I got here. He's getting to be as bad as everyone else, staring at me, waiting for this baby to come."

"When are you due?" Dan asked.

"Not for three weeks."

"Which is an excellent reason," Nick added, "for you to be sitting down."

"I'm tired of sitting. I sit, and Junior thinks that means it's kick-off time. I'd rather move around." She extended her hand to him again. "It was a pleasure meeting you, Dan. If you'll excuse me, I'm going to sample another one of Maile's coconut fritters."

"Ah. I tried one. Definitely worth abandoning us for."

As casually as he could, he let his gaze drift to the spot where he'd last seen Maddie. Only she was no longer there. Looking about, he took in the casual decor, the growing crowd of people and knew he was in trouble when his heart did a backflip at the sight of Maddie in the opposite corner from where she'd been standing earlier. When he realized Maddie and Carolyn were chatting, his heartbeat took off at a frantic gallop.

It took a couple of deep breaths to squelch his first reaction. Even though there was no reason for the two women not to visit and laugh together, somehow the idea left him more than uncomfortable. It wasn't like he'd done anything inappropriate. Or that Maddie knew enough about him to share some less-than-flattering history with his newfound daughter. And it certainly beat having Carolyn surrounded by a flock of men. All he had to do was keep up with the friendly conversation about fast cars, fast boats and pregnant women. And find an excuse to stroll over and casually say hello to Maddie.

"Captain."

Dan spun about to see Yvette Harper approaching.

"I thought that was you. What a nice surprise."

Smiling at the pleasant woman, he pointed a thumb at her son. "I've been getting reacquainted with a couple of my star pupils."

"I didn't realize you were EOD." Yvette slanted a prideful glance at her son, then immediately shifted her attention back to Dan. "What a happy coincidence you should meet up here."

"Dan has been catching us up with his career." Nick slung an arm about his mom. "Most recently he'd been working with marine mammal operational systems out of Point Loma."

"Point Loma? Isn't that in San Diego?"

Dan nodded. "It is."

"My daughter lives in San Diego. Isn't it a small world?"

"Isn't it though." *And his world was getting smaller every minute.*

Maddie found herself searching Carolyn's face, looking for similarities with her father—the man Maddie had not expected to ever see again but now was almost giddy at a chance to spend more time with. Dan had said very little about his daughter that day in Honolulu. Right away the one thing that struck Maddie was the woman's smile. Definitely her father's. Warm and welcoming. She probably would have made a great elementary school teacher. Or even a Realtor.

"Is this a private party, or can anyone join in?" Kara snatched a cream puff from a nearby table.

Angela waved her over. "The more the merrier. I want you to meet Kona's newest resident, Carolyn Porter."

Quickly Kara shoved the entire puff into her mouth and moaned with delight. "Maile should so open her own bakery." Extending her hand, Kara introduced herself to the only unfamiliar person in the group. "Sorry, lately food always distracts me. Kara Harper."

"You've got a great excuse." Carolyn returned the handshake. "Did you say, *Harper*?"

"She's married to my brother, Nick."

"Ah, so *this*"—Carolyn tipped her head in Kara's direction—"is the reason the whole family has come to Kona."

"Most of the reason." An impish grin passed across Maddie's face. "We're pretty fond of Nick too."

Kara smiled at her sister-in-law's comment, placing both her hands on her protruding belly. "It seems pretty obvious I'm fond of him as well."

The four women laughed, then moved on to chatting about the benefits and disadvantages of living on an island plus Carolyn's hunt for the perfect affordable home. The entire time, while sampling more of Maile's treats, Kara kept one hand perched on her tummy. Maddie couldn't begin to fathom how uncomfortable it must be to carry around the equivalent of a twenty-pound bowling ball in front of you 24/7.

"So, how are you enjoying your new house?" Kara asked, popping another cream puff into her mouth.

"Loving it. Not too big, not too small. And while I do miss the fall colors of Tennessee, it doesn't compare with living in paradise."

That was what Maddie had always thought about San Diego. Not too hot, not too cold, the beach practically at her doorstep, and, if she couldn't find what she needed at home, L.A. was only a short drive away. But San Diego was lacking the one thing Kona had—family.

With an eye on her brother and Dan, Maddie did her best to keep up with the changing conversation. All set to excuse herself and meander in Dan's direction, she saw Maile, accompanied by an attractive redhead, smother Dan in a motherly hug, and then slip away leaving Dan and the redhead side by side in conversation. Biting down on her back teeth, Maddie did her best to ignore the churning in her gut, and the urge to storm across the room and hip-check the redhead. How absurd was that? Maddie had been dating Gary from her office exclusively for almost three months when she'd caught him and his bimbo in a less-than-platonic clench, and Maddie had barely flinched. Now she felt like a jealous mate over a man she'd only spent a few sightseeing hours with.

"Don't you agree?"

Three sets of eyes staring at Maddie suggested not only had she completely tuned out the conversation but apparently she was supposed to agree with something. "Sorry, what was that?"

Angela smiled up at her as though ignoring them was no big deal. "It would be nice if her father relocated here instead of stateside."

"I don't know. Where does he live now?"

"He was stationed in San Diego working with the marine mammal program. My father was in explosive ordinance disposal like your brother was. He loves working with the marine program, but it's scheduled for shut down, and I don't think he would appreciate a desk job anywhere else. So he decided to just get out as soon as he hit his twenty years rather than stay in for another ten."

"Do you think he would have stayed if the program

weren't ending?"

Carolyn shrugged. "I don't honestly know."

Across the room Maddie caught a glimpse of Dan heading into the house. "If you'll excuse me a minute?"

Her friends nodded and fell back into discussing the pros versus cons of living near parents. Once inside, Maddie surveyed the area. Several small groups of people milled about, laughing, drinking and, of course, munching on Maile's great cooking. But no sign of the man she was looking for. Skirting around a few people she recognized from the dive shop, she maneuvered her way into the kitchen. Bingo. Straightening up from pulling a beer out of the cooler stood the object of her interest.

"Hey." She moved beside him and reached for a bottled water in a nearby cooler.

"Here, let me." Bending over at the same moment, their heads bumped, and both sprang erect. "Sorry. I should have seen that coming." Dan inched closer, raising his hand in her direction for a moment and then let it fall to his side. "You okay?"

Rubbing her temple she looked at him with one eye open. "I didn't think anyone had a harder head than my brother."

"I can get you a bag of ice."

"That won't be necessary." She let her hand drop even though she wanted to rub the spot a bit more. "I'm fine."

"Okay, but if you wake up with a knot on your head, I don't want your brother coming after me. I'm getting too old for brawls."

"According to my brother a sailor is never too old for a good brawl. Especially if they're brawling with jarheads."

A crooked grin teased at one side of his mouth. "Maybe then."

"Maybe then what?" Kara walked in to set an empty plate on the counter.

"The age-old tradition of squid versus jarhead." Dan opened the nearest cooler. "Can I offer you something to drink?"

"A water would be nice. I think I totally overindulged in

those cream puffs, but I'm pretty sure I can blame the indigestion on the coconut fritters." Kara rubbed her tummy with one hand and accepted the cool bottle of water with the other. "Thanks. I'm going to make my husband happy and find a comfy chair to sit in."

"Do you need something else? Maybe warm tea would be better?" Maddie suggested.

"Nope. Going to get off my feet and stop munching my way through the house. See ya." Kara tipped the bottle at Dan and Maddie, and waddled out of the kitchen.

"They seem like a really nice couple. Billy and his wife too." Dan's gaze returned to Maddie.

"You know what they say. Life is what happens while you're busy making other plans."

Leaning back against the counter, he crossed his ankles and took a sip of his beer.

Maddie watched the reflexive motion of his throat as he swallowed. He set down the drink, and her gaze followed a path from his lengthy fingers still wrapped around the longneck bottle, up strong arms and broad shoulders, across a firm square jaw to settle on the sparkling green eyes that had her captivated with an interest she hadn't felt in so long she'd actually forgotten what infatuation was like.

If she didn't stop looking at him that way, he was going to forget she was too young for him, forget who her brother was and forget why ignoring those things would be a really bad idea.

Good sense must have been smiling on him. Before he had time to decide anything, a swarm of people seemed to descend on the kitchen, one after the other. Groups of two and three, all suddenly searching for another drink, more napkins, a bottle opener. By the time Billy's sister Emily came hurrying inside in search of another spatula, Dan decided he was simply in the way. He leaned into Maddie, close enough to notice she used a vanilla-scented shampoo.

"I think it's time for a little fresh air."

Maddie bobbed her head and led the way through the increasingly crowded kitchen out to a charming gazebo in the back corner of the yard.

"Lovely spot here."

"Every place seems to be a lovely spot."

Leaning against the railing, he took in the tropical yard. "I can see why Carolyn didn't want to go back to Tennessee after college."

"How did she wind up attending college in Honolulu in the first place?"

"She didn't come right out and tell me, but I believe she followed a boy."

"That's a heck of a long way to go for a boyfriend."

"It's a long way to go for anyone." Just then he caught site of Kara walking toward the back end of the ample lawn. Keeping her in his line of site, he shifted to face Maddie. "Looks like the baby's going to be coming pretty soon."

"Three weeks."

Shaking his head, he cleared his throat to hide a chuckle. "I don't think so."

"What makes you say that?"

"Eight nieces and nephews." He took another sip of his drink. "Not that I was around for all their births. But I was home for two of my nieces' arrivals. My sisters Mary and Liz were like chipmunks storing nuts for winter. The look on both their faces all the way to the delivery room was exactly like the expression on Kara's face just now. And I should know. I drove Liz to the hospital. Thought for sure I'd have to put my emergency medical training to the test on the side of the road."

"What look?"

"It's a cross between heartburn and surrender. Hard to explain, but, if you look at Kara, she's got it."

"You seem pretty sure of yourself."

"Wait till you've been around as long as I have. You learn a lot from reading between the lines."

Maddie tilted her head to one side. "You have a thing about age, don't you?"

"Nope. It is what it is."

"What is that?"

"I'm a forty-two-year-old retired naval officer who is tired of blowing things up for a living and ready for a little more serenity in my life."

"And how do you plan to do that?"

Hefting a shoulder in a casual shrug, he said, "Originally I'd planned on going back to school."

"Originally?"

"The marine mammal program proved to be more fascinating than I'd expected. Several years back I decided to pursue marine biology. Over the years I've gotten my masters. A PhD is my logical next step."

"Uncle Sam let you take a break for a master's degree?"

He shook his head. "Online distance learning is everywhere. And some are very accommodating to the military."

"You sound unsure now."

So much had changed in the last year. "The marine mammal program is being defunded. That requires a new start in a new field. Not easy at my age."

"But you retired anyway?"

He didn't mind teaching, and the navy training programs always involved a lot of action. But with his new pay grade, a desk was more likely in his future, and he'd have hated that. "It was time."

"Did Carolyn have anything to do with the decision to leave the navy?"

The pretty lady didn't beat around the bush. "Let's say she was the final piece of a complex puzzle."

Maddie gave him a knowing smile that seemed to quietly say, *I thought so*. He saw wisdom in those bourbon-colored eyes that made him want to learn everything she knew. When a dark storm dampened the normal sparkle in her eyes, Dan followed her gaze across the yard. A deep ridge made itself at home between her brows.

And then he saw it. Kara, alone, hesitating and then the plate falling from her hand. She swayed forward, not quite doubled over, one hand leaning on the German shepherd at her feet, the other pressing into her side. No one else seemed to notice her or the dropped dish of food on the ground. Taking off at a fast clip, he shouted over his shoulder. "Find your brother. Now."

CHAPTER TEN

Maddie had never been so scared in her life. Not when she went on her first date with the captain of the football team, not her first day at UCLA, not when she wrote her first real estate contract and not even every time an airplane took off or landed. Logic told her that nothing was wrong; women had babies every day. Even three weeks early. But that didn't stop the adrenaline rush that had her sprinting across the yard like she'd been prodded by a pitchfork.

"Oops." Emily, Billy's sister, almost collided with Maddie at the patio doorway.

"I need Nick."

Emily's eyes rounded, the whites of her eyes forming a perfect ring around the darkened centers. "Kara?"

Scanning the inside of the house, Maddie nodded.

"I saw him and Billy going out the front door with Jonathan. Something about his new motorcycle. Where is she?"

"Outside near the bench by the rose garden. I'll go out front. You hit the kitchen."

"Gotcha."

The two tore off in opposite directions. Maddie ripped open the front door with such force it bounced off the wall. On the curb she saw her brother's best friend and their young employee from the dive shop with a few more people she didn't know. But no Nick and no motorcycle. *Crap.*

Running to the group, she whipped out her cell phone and hit speed dial. Breathless, the phone at her ear, she grabbed Billy by the arm. "Where's Nick?"

"He took Jonathan's bike for a test run. What's wrong?"

"It's Kara." Her brother's blasted cell went to voice mail. "I think she's in labor."

"If you're calling him, he's not going to hear the ring tone with the helmet on." He lifted his gaze toward the house. "Where is she?"

"In the backyard. Dan is with her. Emily is searching inside for Nick."

Facing her full-on, Billy put a hand on each of her shoulders. "Take a deep breath and wait here for Nick. Hopefully he won't be taking a very long spin." Then Billy inhaled a long breath himself and spun on his heel, racing into the house.

Even though she knew there was no point, she stabbed again at the phone. Willing Nick to answer. "Come on, big brother."

From halfway across the yard Dan could see Kara's pale complexion. The woman was most definitely in labor. Or in trouble.

"Hey there." He slowed his approach speed. "Need some help?"

"It felt stuffy in the house. I thought I'd come sit out here in the garden and enjoy a slice of my mother-in-law's pie." Kara sucked in a long breath and blew it out slowly.

"Can you straighten?" He wrapped an arm around her waist; the dog at their feet nudged his hand with its muzzle. "It's okay, boy. She's fine."

"*She* probably should have quit eating two coconut fritters ago. And to answer your question, the pain in my side gets sharper when I stand up. I think I pulled something."

"I doubt that. Any other pain?"

She shook her head. "Just a little indigestion. I really should stop eating, but it's all so good."

"How long have you had the indigestion?"

"I guess since the pizza last night. I shouldn't do tomato

sauce either."

"Last night?" Holy cow this woman has been in labor almost a full day. No wonder the pain wouldn't stop; she had to be in the last stages of labor. "Kara, we need to get you to a hospital."

She hissed through gritted teeth, leaning forward more heavily on his arm, and then slowly eased her grip. "Oh, that hurt."

"I'm going to assume, if you can't straighten, you can't walk either?"

Eyes closed, she nodded her head. "Good guess. You go to the front of the class."

He actually chuckled. The woman still had her sense of humor. Nick had done well for himself. "I'm going to slip my arms under you and pick you up. Okay?"

"I'm going to break your back."

He laughed again. "No, you're not. Just hang on to my neck." Hooking his arms under her, he hefted her up against him. "See? Light as a feather."

"Liar, liar, pants on ..." She huffed out a breath. "... fire."

Moving as quickly as he dared with Kara in his arms, Dan was extremely grateful that, even though he hadn't been on the field with heavy equipment in years, he'd kept in shape nonetheless. "We're almost to the house." And he certainly hoped her husband was there and ready to take over. Though he had some serious doubts that this baby wouldn't be born in the backseat of the car.

Nearly to the house Billy and his mother came running toward him. Billy didn't say a word; he just looked Dan in the eye. The question was there for any team member to read. Is there a problem? And with a single blink of his eyes and a nearly imperceptible nod, Billy had his phone out and punching numbers. Dan's guess ... 9-1-1.

By now half the guests were scrambling about, some steering clear, others moving in closer. "I don't suppose anyone here is a doctor or a nurse."

"Dr. Shepherd," Maile called, hurrying over to the couch, a blanket and pillow in hand.

"He already left." Emily came rushing behind her mother. "But he's a psychiatrist. What does he know about babies?"

Maile dropped the linens on a nearby chair. "A psychiatrist is an MD. He has to know more about this than any of us do."

"Where's Nick?" Dan leaned at the edge of the couch eager to determine if he needed to put Kara down or continue out to the car.

Jonathan came trotting in the front door. "Nick's coming down the street. Madeleine's waiting for him." The kid took one look at Kara wincing in Dan's arms and teetered in place before scurrying back outside.

Billy slid his phone into his pocket. "An ambulance is on the way."

"How long will that take?"

"Ten minutes."

Kara's grip squeezed his bicep for the third time since he'd lifted her into his arms. Not a good sign. Dan looked to the blankets on the chair. At three weeks early he'd rather have a tank of oxygen handy. "I don't think we've got the luxury of time."

Nick came hurtling through the door and nearly tumbled over the ottoman by the coffee table before skidding to a halt in front of her, his sister on his heels. "Are you all right?"

"Ask an easier quest … ion." Kara's whole face scrunched tightly.

Nick's gaze flew to Dan's. Too many questions to decipher flickered in his worried eyes. Dan could pretty much imagine every one of them. Is this normal? Is it too early? How much time do we have? I can't lose her. Them. What do I do, Captain?

"How far is the hospital?" Dan asked.

"Maybe fifteen minutes."

"Contractions seem to be only a few minutes apart. She's close."

"That's not how it's supposed to work." Nick looked at his wife's pinched face. "The first baby is supposed to give us plenty of time. In three weeks."

Kara lifted her head up. "Stop squawking, and get me to the car."

"I'd better move my car. I'm blocking the driveway." A tall skinny guy ran out the door.

"Oh, no. We're behind Nick's car." Angela looked about. "Where's my purse? The keys are in my purse."

Different people began pulling car keys out of pockets and handbags, and making their way outside. Dan could hear Billy in the front yard already shouting orders at different people to move their cars here and there.

"I'd feel better if we had medical staff handy." Dan took in a deep breath. "I'm not a doctor, and I have no idea if you'll make it to the hospital. But I wouldn't count on it."

Nick nodded. Looked to his wife.

Kara grabbed and squeezed his hand. "Ambulance is only a few minutes away. We'll wait." She tried to smile, but another contraction grabbed hold of her.

Without being told, Maile spread the blanket on the couch. Dan eased Kara onto the sofa. Nick's mother appeared out of nowhere with the pillow and silently stuffed it behind Kara's back, then retreated out of sight. Emily pushed a chair closer to the sofa and practically shoved Nick into it. Madeleine turned and ran, shouting over her shoulder, "I'll tell the Indy 500 crew we're waiting on the ambulance."

With everyone tripping over themselves to either help or get out of the way, Maddie's ability to just step in to do what was needed, and joke about it at the same time, only frustrated him more. If after all these years he had finally found a woman who'd wormed her way under his skin, why the heck did it have to be someone so young?

"Ooh." Kara bit down hard, her grunts and groan taking on a more unnerving decibel.

Easing out of the way, Dan leaned over so only Maile and Yvette Harper could hear him. "Just in case, we could use some towels. I'll see if any of the men have shoelaces. But it might be time to clear everyone out of here."

Maile took off like a shot down the hall. Yvette quietly

began ushering folks out onto the patio. Emily and Angela repositioned food trays from the dining table to outdoors. A couple of the guys grabbed a cooler each and carried them outside as well. Dan walked among the guests, glancing down at their feet, thrilled to spot a young woman in crisp, clean running shoes. "Those new?"

"Yeah." She grinned up at him. "Got them for a steal yesterday at a going-out-of-business sale. Couldn't wait to break them in."

"They look really nice. Would you mind very much if I took your laces?"

The way her brows flew up and she swayed backward, Dan knew she was debating if Maile had any psychos on the guest list.

"We might need them to tie the cord."

"Oh." Before he could say anything else, she was crouching on the ground unlacing her shoes, careful not to let them touch the ground.

Back inside, Dan glanced around at the empty room. Only Nick and Kara on the sofa. His mother at the back door. Maile at the front. The two women standing guard. If Dan were still running a navy EOD team, he wouldn't mind having either of these two women on it.

Just then Kara blurted out, "I want to push."

"No," Dan said as calmly as he could. "Breathe through it. The ambulance will be here any minute."

Nick began murmuring words of encouragement, wiping her brow, pausing to pant with her. Dan had lost track of time when he heard the approaching ambulance's sirens grow closer. In his career he'd needed to draw on his emergency medical training too many times, for too many horrible reasons. But never had he been more relieved than having just been spared putting to the test his long-ago classes on birthing a baby.

CHAPTER ELEVEN

Staring at the ambulance's taillights dwindling in the distance, Maddie's feet felt rooted to the ground. Even now with Kara safely on her way to the hospital, Maddie's heart still banged a savage beat against her rib cage.

"Everything will be fine." Her mom stood behind her, soft hands gliding up and down Maddie's upper arms in a soothing motion. "Let's go on inside and get our things. We don't want the baby to arrive before we get to the hospital."

Tense muscles barely afforded her enough strength to bob her head. Yvette slowly stepped back, turned and led the way into the house. Maddie was only slightly surprised to see Dan standing a few feet away, waiting for her. The guy had orchestrated things like the commanding officer he'd recently been. And he'd called it earlier too. Predicted the baby wasn't going to wait three weeks. Had said Kara had that look. For a guy who had never been married or had newborns of his own, he certainly understood pregnant women.

"Your mother's right. Everything will work out," he reassured.

And wasn't it nice of him to realize she needed reassuring. Maddie nodded again, and, lifting feet that felt shoed in concrete, she walked beside him. "You were wonderful back there. When the rest of us were running like chickens with our heads cut off, you kept your cool."

He chuckled softly. "Comes with the territory. Besides, we undergo an enormous amount of training for EOD, including emergency medicine."

"So the navy expects you guys to deliver babies while

disarming bombs?"

"Not exactly. But we like to be prepared." He flashed her a broad smile. "Just in case."

"Well, you were certainly prepared. You had everything down, from the towels to the shoelace."

"Oh, the navy didn't teach me that." He opened the front door for her. "I learned it from a Doris Day movie."

Maddie walked past him into the house. She had no idea if he was serious or not, but the way his eyes twinkled with laughter, she had no choice but to smile back.

Rubbing her hands together with glee, Maile surveyed the living area. "I just love babies. Emily, help me put a few of these things that will spoil in to the fridge."

"Can I help?" Carolyn asked.

"Absolutely." Maile waved toward the door. "You can start bringing in the food from outside."

"I'll give you a hand," Angela said to Carolyn.

"And since you know most everyone, Angela, start suggesting folks either go on home or head over to the hospital if they want to see the new baby."

"Shouldn't we just send them all home?" Carolyn asked.

"Nah. Around here a new baby is bigger news than a tsunami. Folks who know Nick and Kara will show up at the hospital no matter what we say, and, when the baby comes, Nick will be strutting around like a young rooster who figured out how to crow."

"I can help a minute." Yvette picked up a platter of deviled eggs.

"Nonsense. Grammas, grampas, aunts and uncles don't clean the kitchen. They get their keisters to the hospital. Now scoot."

"But—"

Maile made shooing motions with her hands. "No buts. Out you go, all of you. And I'll make sure Margaret takes Bradley home with her. The boys can play until Bradley's brother or sister gets here. Then Margaret or Sara can bring them to meet the new addition to the family."

From a chair in the corner, Maddie retrieved her purse.

"I'll dri..." *Crud.* "We came with Nick. He's got the car keys."

Emily looked up. "I can take you. Just let me stash this in the fridge, and we—"

"I'll take them." Dan held up a set of keys. "You stay. The more folks helping here, the sooner your mom can get to the hospital."

Maile's face bloomed into a broad smile worthy of a vacation poster. "Thank you, Carolyn's nice father."

"Do you know where we're going?" Maddie slung her purse over her shoulder.

"Nope, but James the GPS does." Dan gave her a full-blown smile that almost made her forget how anxious she was.

"If you don't mind"—her hands filled with two trays from outside, Carolyn paused in front of her dad—"I'll catch a ride later with someone else."

Only a few steps behind Carolyn, Angela spoke up. "Billy and I will take you."

"We can too," Emily offered.

This was what Maddie was lacking in San Diego. When she'd left Texas, she'd been thrilled to escape the claustrophobic feeling of everyone in her life and her business. Not until now did she realize how much she had missed the support system that came with it.

Dan nodded at everyone, smiled at his daughter and, twenty minutes later, he and the remaining Harpers all piled out of his rental and into the hospital.

"I'm looking for my daughter-in-law, Kara Harper."

The nurse behind the large emergency room reception desk clacked away at the keyboard.

"They couldn't have been too far ahead of us. The ambulance just brought her in."

"Oh." The woman looked up from the screen. "Here she is. They've just now taken her upstairs to maternity. Third floor. Elevators are down the hall to your left."

"Thank you."

The silence in the elevator spoke volumes for how concerned everyone was. Normally Maddie's bubbly mother would be prattling on with excitement over the new grandbaby, but instead the weight of a premature birth stilled her and the others' tongues. The moment the doors opened, Yvette flew to the nurses' station. "My daughter-in-law was just brought up. Kara Harper."

"Let me see." The older nurse glanced at a white erase board behind her. "I don't see ..."

"She's having a baby," Yvette said so simply, without recognition of how blatantly unnecessary the comment was in the maternity ward that, for the first time in what seemed like hours, Maddie had to smother a smile.

When the nurse turned slowly, looking over the rim of her glasses at Yvette, Maddie had to cover her mouth to stop from laughing out loud.

"Everyone gets a little nervous when a baby is coming." Dan bit back a grin, his lips turned slightly upward at the corners.

Another bank of elevator doors opened, and a handful of people Maddie recognized from the party came out and huddled behind her mother, asking about Kara and the baby.

"Mrs. Harper has been moved to a delivery room. If you will all take a seat in the visitors' lounge, I'm sure someone will be out shortly to give you an update."

Obediently everyone marched down the hall to the waiting area. Holding hands, her parents chose to walk back and forth. Maddie commandeered a spot in the corner. Dan took a seat beside her. Every few minutes another person or two showed up, and soon the chatter in the room had grown as loud and happy as the atmosphere at the party had been.

All Maddie wanted was for Nick and Kara to have a healthy baby. And an update.

"I'm sure someone will be out soon."

For a moment she asked herself if Dan could possibly read her mind. "I was just thinking I wished someone would give us an update."

"I know." She must have looked totally bewildered because he added, "You keep casting furtive glances down the hall."

Was her brother that observant? This man seemed to be aware of everything around him. And totally capable of handling any sudden change. Not many people could read each other with just one look. "You really are something. Or do women tell you that all the time?"

Dan chuckled lightly. "I've been called a *something* or two."

"So how have you stayed out of some woman's snare all this time?"

"You overestimate my appeal."

"Nonsense. My brother was in the navy too. Remember? I am fully aware of the effect a nice summer white uniform has on the ladies. And the not-so-ladylike."

He chuckled again. "I'm well past the age of impressing women with my uniform."

"What is it with you and age? You make it sound like you've got one foot in the grave and the other on a banana peel."

"I wouldn't go that far. But reaching eligibility for retirement after twenty years of service reminds a man that not being able to eat as much as he used to without adding an extra set of reps to his workout routine has more to do with his age than the additives in his diet. Then finding yourself at the same time no longer a steadfast bachelor but the father of a full-grown daughter can certainly make you take a long look at yourself. And that long look can be painful."

"First of all there *is* a lot of crap in our foods making us fat. Second, I would think being eligible to retire at only forty-two-years *young* is a good thing. And lastly, it's not like Carolyn showed up with a bunch of grandchildren in tow. She's barely out of school. That's still pretty young."

"Says the pot to the kettle."

"I beg your pardon?"

"You've got a couple of decades before you've got to deal with a slowing metabolism, strained muscles and fading eyesight."

"Not hardly."

Rubber soles squeaking on the tile floor announced the nurse scampering down the hall and headed for the waiting area. The petite woman grew closer, and Maddie found herself pushing to her feet. Dan stood as well, and, all of a sudden, as the woman stood at the doorway looking around the crowded room, Maddie felt the warmth of a strong hand enfold hers. She hadn't noticed when she'd done it, but she must have extended her hand to him, and, without fuss or fanfare, he'd taken it in his.

"Mr. and Mrs. Harper?"

Maddie's parents moved in closer. "That's us."

"If you'll come with me, your son has someone to introduce you to."

The room exploded in a raucous cheer. High fives, hoots, hollers, hugs and kisses were exchanged with gusto. Maddie spun about and flung her arms around Dan. She veered north, and he leaned south. Intending to kiss him on the cheek, their lips met, and the world stopped.

This was so not what Dan had in mind when her arms flew around his neck. A quick peck on the cheek. A felicitation for the safe arrival of her brother's child. Not the heat of pliable soft lips against his.

Inching away and looking into her eyes, the same startled reaction he'd had now stared back at him. But more dangerous, and more enticing, was the yearning in those eyes. The smoky haze of desire cut through him as clearly as if she'd held a knife to his gut. Her lips barely parted, maybe to speak, maybe to breathe, it didn't matter. His mouth cut her off. Perfection creating a unique touch that somehow seemed so familiar.

The deep rumble of a man laughing nearby penetrated the haze in Dan's mind, and, as quickly as the kiss had come to be, they pulled apart. Now he'd done it. Dragging his gaze away from Maddie's, he glanced quickly around the room. It didn't appear anyone had noticed his misstep. Carolyn was engrossed in conversation with Angela. Maile, her friend Margaret and a few others were literally bouncing with excitement. And all he wanted was to kiss Madeleine Harper again.

CHAPTER TWELVE

"Look who we have here," Yvette Harper announced.

All heads turned in her direction. Nick stood by the entryway, cradling a bundle in a yellow blanket, his mother beaming at his side. "I would like to introduce you to Catherine Grace Harper. Six pounds, five ounces and nineteen inches of beautiful healthy baby girl."

Like bees returning to the hive, every breathing person in the room swarmed around him, doing what all normal people did with new babies—they made silly noises and even sillier faces and all-around fools of themselves. And no one cared.

And while Maddie knew she should be front and center, making the biggest fool over her new niece, she couldn't get over the one very brief and very thorough kiss from retired US Navy Captain Daniel O'Neil.

Fingertips to her lips, she managed to move her feet, taking a step back. "I have to go."

Smoky green eyes remained fixed on her. Eyes that seemed to be swimming in the same sensation overload as her. Only the sound of his voice had her dragging her gaze away from his.

"Congratulations."

"Thank you." Whether she meant for the comment or the kiss, even she wasn't sure. Finally managing to spin about, she almost smacked into her brother. So consumed by the heat of the moment, she hadn't heard him walk up behind her.

A smile as wide and big as the island covered his face, but rather than his gaze gleaming with the high of the moment, his eyes drilled into Dan—a conversation she wasn't able to decipher. But when Dan took a step back, she guessed he understood her brother perfectly.

"Catherine, I'd like you to meet your aunt Madeleine." He passed off the tiny baby.

"I have handbags that weigh more than you do." Catherine Grace lifted an arm and snuggled into the embrace. "Oh, she's beautiful."

"Looks like her mama." Yvette ran one finger along the tiny girl's jaw, and little Catherine Grace immediately opened her mouth. "I think we need to get this angel back to her mother."

"Good idea." Nick nodded. "Why don't you do that?"

"You don't have to ask me twice to hold my grandbaby." With an ease that would have led anyone watching to believe Yvette was a seasoned grandmother, she swooped the baby out of Maddie's arms and made her way back to Kara's hospital room, cooing and chatting, and promising her first granddaughter everything from cooking lessons to tiaras.

"Here you go." Billy slapped Nick on the back and handed him a small box with a wide painted bow and the words *It's a Girl* across the top. "Picked these up downstairs. Thought they might come in handy."

Her brother opened the lid and barked out a laugh. Chocolate cigars. "How'd you know she would be a girl? None of us knew."

Shoulders straight and smiling like everyone else on the floor, Billy tipped his head toward his wife coming his way. "The boy box is in her handbag."

That made Nick laugh even louder. That was Billy, always prepared.

Dan stuck his hand out to her brother. "Congratulations. She's beautiful."

"Thank you." Nick took his hand, and it looked to Maddie like the handshake and the eye contact lasted much longer than normal. They were communicating again.

And she was pretty darn sure whatever her brother was telling him, she wasn't going to like it. "How's Kara doing?"

"Great." Nick let go of Dan's hand and spun to face his sister. "She's exhausted. Apparently she'd been in labor since last night and didn't realize it."

Maddie leaned back, her entire face scrunched up. "How could that be?"

"She thought she couldn't sleep because of indigestion. She was having mostly back labor, a little heartburn, and here we are."

"The important thing is, everyone is healthy and happy," Dan interjected.

"There's no problem that she's a few weeks early?" Maddie asked.

Nick shook his head. "She's perfectly fine. Everything tests within normal range, and six-and-a-half pounds for a first baby is a good size. The doctor said, if Kara had gone to term, she'd have probably delivered an eight-pound butterball."

"When can I see your wife?" Maddie asked.

"Now, if you want, but she was actually dosing off. That's why Mom and I brought the baby out here."

"In that case, give me your keys, and I'll go get the car so you have wheels to go home in."

Patting his pants pocket, Nick looked down, then up. "How did you get here?"

"I brought her and your parents," Dan spoke up.

Nick slanted him another studious glance. "I see."

"Hand them over." Maddie opened her palm.

"Here you go, but the SUV is new. Let Dad drive."

"Are you never going to let me forget?" Maddie grabbed the keys. Dan looked from her to Nick and back.

"Nope." Nick flashed a cheesy grin, then turned to Dan. "This is the woman who took too close to heart the old adage *bumpers were meant to be bumped.* Apparently her driver's ed teacher failed to explain today's bumpers aren't metal barricades but plastic-covered Styrofoam."

"One lousy bump." She rolled her eyes.

Nick ignored her and looked back to Dan. "She took out the neighbor's fence."

Dan's eyes widened, amusement flickering.

"I was learning how to drive, and the phone was ringing."

"Not a confidence builder. You're a Realtor now. Your phone rings all the time. Remember the rear taillight?"

"There was ice! I can't be blamed for Mother Nature. Texans aren't taught how to drive on ice." Maddie faced Dan. "My senior year of college he let me use his car for a ski vacation over the winter break with some friends near Colorado Springs. We hit a patch of ice. I fishtailed *and* saved us from crashing into other cars, but the taillight tapped a light post."

Doing a lousy job of hiding his smile, Dan shrugged and addressed Nick. "She has a point. It's a pain to drive on ice."

"What about the car door at the—"

"That's enough." Maddie lifted her hand in front of her, palm out. "I'll go get Dad."

"If I may make a suggestion?" Dan reached for her arm, and the electricity immediately zapped her. "If the lieutenant here is serious, why don't I take you back to the house? You can drive the rental, and I'll follow you in the SUV, and your father can stay with your mom and the baby." He turned to Nick. "That is if you trust my driving."

"To hell and back, sir." Another one of those long, intense looks that spoke tomes passed between the two men before Nick faced his sister. "You're too easy to tease. Let the captain give you a lift, then bring me my car. I don't know how late I'll be, but at least you guys will have wheels."

"Okay." Except now she was going to be alone with the best kisser she'd ever known and had no idea what to do about it.

The walk from the waiting room to the elevator had been a pitiful example of polite conversation focusing on the arrival of Miss Catherine Grace Harper. Mostly because

Dan was too chicken to discuss what was really on his mind. Wanting more from Madeleine Harper.

He'd spent a handful of hours with this smart lady, and, with every new thing he learned about her, he wanted to know much much more. He knew she was bright and sassy and pretty and caring and a little klutzy.

"How old *are* you?" There. He'd asked the question. Put the dirty-old-man card on the table.

"Excuse me?" The elevator doors opened, and Maddie stepped first into the lobby.

"I asked, how old are you?" He knew she had to be at least a little older than his daughter since he knew Maddie had graduated from UCLA and sold real estate in San Diego. And from what she'd shared about her work, he got the impression that she'd had enough time to establish a solid reputation.

She stopped in the middle of the lobby and looked up at him. "Why?"

"I just wanted to know."

Maddie continued walking out of the building. "Thirty."

Thirty. His heart gave his rib cage a small fist bump. Somehow thirty sounded so much older than twenty-nine. And way better than the twenty-five or so that he'd imagined her to be. But that still left twelve years between them. Not exactly robbing the cradle.

At thirty that would have made Madeleine eight when his daughter was born. Not that he'd been long into adulthood when Carolyn was born, but Maddie was still in elementary school. Had he met her fifteen years ago, what he was thinking of doing with her now would have been a criminal offense in most, if not all, fifty states.

"It's no big deal." Shading her eyes from the sun with her hand, she paused almost at the car to look into his eyes. "There's no ick factor here. No one will look at you and think dirty old man, and they won't see me as a trophy wife." She dropped her hand and shrugged. "Not that we're talking marriage here, just saying."

Was that what he wanted? After all these years as a bachelor? Could that be why the age thing bothered him so much? He wasn't thinking of Maddie for a port stop, but as home port?

Pointing the fob at his car, he clicked and opened the door, waited for her to settle inside, closed the door, skirted around to the driver side and climbed in. Staring at the steering wheel a moment, he sucked in a long breath and mentally stepped back. Only twelve years. Slowly he wrapped his mind around the idea that he was not technically old enough to be her father. That was something.

Stepping on the brake, he pushed the ignition button. Her back stiff, her jaw clenched, Maddie kept her gaze out the window, and he realized, if he'd managed to push her too far, it wouldn't matter a lick if there was only a thirty-day difference between them. *Blast*, he had less then fifteen minutes between here and the house to make everything right.

Maddie wondered, what was the big deal? He thought he was too old for her. Or she was too young for him. Six of one, half a dozen of the other. The man was an idiot.

Who was she trying to kid. He wasn't even close to an idiot. Gary from the office was a first-class idiot. She'd had a string of idiots in her life. A few nice guys, but mostly idiots. All the way back to the captain of the football team who had thought there wasn't a skirt in the county who didn't want to get friendly with him in the backseat of his souped-up Camaro. "Jerk."

"I'm sorry."

"Oh." She sprang around. "I didn't mean you."

"One of the requirements for my job is to be able to think ahead. Anticipate the unexpected. Be prepared—"

"Expect the best, plan for the worst and prepare to be surprised. Yes, my brother says that all the time."

"Does it help to say I'm pleasantly surprised you're thirty?"

"Then you'll be thrilled to know I'll be thirty-one on my next birthday."

"When is that?"

"Valentine's Day."

"That's next weekend."

She nodded. Her dad had bought into the baby pool predicting Catherine would make an early appearance and share Maddie's birthday. Funny how two weeks early had seemed so normal, and yet this morning the idea of three weeks premature had sent most of her family into a silent panic.

He turned the corner to Maile's house. "Do you have plans?"

"We were planning to play it by ear with the baby and all."

"Would you consider joining me for dinner?"

Maddie tugged at her shoulder belt and shifted to face him. "On Valentine's Day?"

He nodded and pulled over to the curb in front of Maile's. "Yes. On Valentine's Day. And your birthday. And a chance to prove I'm not a jerk."

"I wasn't talking about y—"

Placing his finger on her lips, he smiled. "I know. But I'd like that chance anyway." Without waiting for a response, he spun out of his seat and circled the hood in time to open her door for her and offer his hand. "Had enough time to think it over?"

One foot out of the car she pushed from her seat with the other a little too hard and toppled into his arms. Grinning up, she wondered if falling into his arms was going to be a habit with them.

CHAPTER THIRTEEN

Dan had been looking forward to tonight all week. His daughter had helped him plan the perfect date. And, much to his surprise, she'd been better than okay with him dating a younger woman.

"It's not like she's eighteen or something. I mean, what's the big deal?"

Since his PhD program didn't start till summer and things were going really well getting to know his daughter, and Madeleine, Angela—or as Carolyn called her, the Realtor extraordinaire—arranged for him to rent a condo instead of a hotel, at least for a couple more weeks.

But first he had to survive a family luncheon at Nick's house. Unlike last week at Maile's where half the island showed up at some point in the afternoon, this was a quiet family event. Well, family by blood and business, since Billy and Angela were invited. And of course he and Carolyn were invited because he was taking Maddie out on a date for her birthday.

Nick hadn't said anything when Maddie had asked to do a family lunch instead of dinner, but Dan had understood the silent message the same as he had in the hospital. Nick might trust Dan to get him from hell and back, but not so much with his sister. At least not yet.

"Dad, relax." Carolyn rolled her eyes at her father, and only after she'd noticed the surprise on his face did she realize what she'd said. "I'm sorry. Is that okay to call you *Dad*?"

Swallowing hard, Dan nodded. "Of course it is." Carolyn was proving to be a bright, friendly, self-confident woman with an amazing business head on her shoulders.

And nothing had made him as happy in his life as hearing the word *Dad* roll off her lips. "I like it."

For the remainder of the short ride to Nick's, Carolyn filled him in on her day yesterday and her date for dinner tonight. Though Dan hadn't met the guy, Carolyn seemed to like him, and Dan was learning to accept the concept of her liking the guy would have to be good enough. But that didn't mean he was permanently surrendering the parental right to torture the man if he messed with his daughter.

"Oh, this is a lovely home." Appreciation shone in her eyes as they pulled into the driveway and she took in the colorful landscape.

It certainly was. Situated on a hillside he could just imagine the view from the backyard. He collected the bouquet of fresh blooms he'd purchased for Kara and the red rose for Maddie, then escorted Carolyn to the door. He'd seen Madeleine almost every day since the baby was born, but this was their first official date, and he was as nervous as a seaman undergoing his first inspection.

The front door opened, and, with the baby in one arm, Yvette waved them in. "Glad you made it. There's enough food in the kitchen to feed the naval fleet. I hope you brought your appetite."

"Absolutely," Dan answered.

"Just a yogurt for breakfast," Carolyn added.

"These are for Kara."

"They're beautiful." Yvette closed the door behind them. "She's on the sofa. Nick is still trying to make her rest, and she's still debating if it's worth life in prison to just kill him and get it over with. So far it's a draw."

"Hey." Madeleine walked up and gave him a short but sweet peck on the cheek. The simple gesture warmed him clear to his toes.

"I brought these for Kara." He held out the flowers. "And this for you."

Her eyes softened, and she took a whiff of the single red rose. "It's beautiful. I'll get a vase. If you'd like, I can take those and put them in a vase as well for Kara."

"Thanks." His gaze was steady on the soft sway of her

hips when he felt the presence behind him.

"I try not to worry about her," Nick said in a low voice meant only for Dan.

"She's worth worrying about."

Nick nodded and stepped up beside him. "I'm not sure how I feel about all this."

Both men continued to follow Maddie's movements in the kitchen. Dan knew her brother had more to say, so he waited Nick out.

"I don't know your intentions."

Dan was tempted to snap to attention and shout, *"Sir, honorable, sir,"* but kept his silence.

"But I do know my sister. She's sensitive and too giving. And she's not stupid. She understands navy men. She'll be good for you."

"I detect a *but*."

Nick nodded. "You've been around the block—all around the world. I'm not convinced you'd be good for her."

Neither was he, but, in the week that had passed, he'd concluded he desperately wanted to try. If he wasn't already in love with Madeleine Harper, he standing on the brim about to topple over. And liking the prospect more than he'd ever thought possible.

"When she arrived here, she was talking about making a move. A permanent move to Kona." Nick leveled his gaze with Dan's. "She's not doing that now. Leaving San Diego doesn't seem to be in her plans anymore."

Dan would be in San Diego for a long while completing his doctorate, and, hopefully when he was done, there would be plenty of opportunities for a man with his background to do what he'd come to love over the last few years. But he'd be lying if he didn't admit he'd considered chucking it all if Maddie did decide to up and move to Hawaii.

Nick cleared his throat. "Superior officer or not, don't make me have to come after you."

"You have my word." Dan didn't have to say more. They both knew what was on the table. None of them were kids anymore. And hearts were fragile, complex organs. At this point, Dan was more worried that Maddie might break his if they moved forward with this relationship and discovered the generation gap was indeed a wider divide than they'd hoped. And right now he was definitely hoping to make whatever they had last a lifetime.

The restaurant was spectacular. Not far up the coastline, it rested on an outcrop of black lava rocks, the water splashing along the lower walls. Dan gave his name, and the waiter led them to a small table in the far corner of the open veranda. A large potted palm to one side gave privacy not afforded the other tables.

The views were wonderful. And the menu mouthwatering. But Maddie was more enthralled with the company.

By the time the waiter had taken their order and served the first courses, conversation had covered everything from Texas armadillos to signs of the zodiac. She'd learned about Dan growing up with seven siblings in Kentucky and things about EOD that her brother had never explained. Things she was happy not to have known when he was still active duty. And Dan's eyes never once glazed over when she'd gone on about office politics, demanding clients or the adverse effects of mortgage insurance premiums. But they'd laughed and joked, and she had never felt more at home with a man in her life.

"Everything was so delicious." Maddie toyed with the last remnants of dessert on her plate.

"The crab bisque was great, and the coconut berry house salad was … interesting."

Biting back a grin, she'd been pretty sure he was a meat-and-potatoes man even before he'd ordered.

"But the ribeye definitely had my name on it."

"Mine too." Slowly savoring the last bite of the blueberry sour cream pie, she set down her fork. "But this is most definitely my favorite part."

"And here I thought you were a carnivore like me."

"I am. Being from Texas, it's practically sacrilegious not to love a good steak. I just appreciate my desserts as well."

The waiter came back a few minutes later with the bill. Dan's John Hancock on the dotted line, he reached for her hand and escorted her out of the place. "You up for a walk?"

"On the beach? Always." Strolling in the moonlight, Maddie debated whether or not to bring up his and Nick's earlier encounter.

"You might as well spit it out."

Stopping in her tracks, her gaze flew up to meet his. "How do you do that?"

"What?"

"Know what I'm thinking?"

"I don't. Otherwise I wouldn't have asked. But I recognize that look. So tell me what's on your mind."

She had a look? She picked up walking again. "Nick."

Dan's brows buckled. "What's the matter with Nick?"

"I saw him talking to you while I was putting the flowers in a vase. It wasn't one of those *How'd you like the game last night* conversations."

"No, it wasn't."

"He was warning you off me. Wasn't he?"

Dan ran his thumb back and forth along her hand. "Not exactly."

"Then what exactly?"

"He was just being a good big brother. Making sure my intentions were, are, honorable."

Maddie could feel the heat in her cheeks. Dan already thought her too young for him, and now Nick was treating her like a teenager on prom night. "Oh, please tell me, he didn't really say that. Did he?"

"Not in so many words." Dan stole a glance at Maddie and smiled. "Relax. He's not loading a shot gun or anything."

Maddie squeezed his hand and shook her head. "If

you're not careful, we may turn into my parents."

His forehead creased, and Maddie noted, rather than concern from before, this time his eyes expressed confusion.

"Pretty soon you'll be reading me so well words won't be required at all."

"Would that be such a bad thing?" He lifted up their entangled hands and repeated, "Would it?"

All she could do was shake her head.

"We're not teenagers."

Thank heaven for that.

"As you're brother didn't hesitate to point out, I've been around the block a time or two."

"Or three," she added playfully.

"Or three," he repeated. "I think we have something special started here."

She nodded.

"More than special."

She nodded again, and this time she saw the change in him. Eyes filled with hesitation were now brimmed with determination—and something else.

"I've been thinking a lot about when we get back to San Diego."

"Hope for the best, plan for the worst," she teased, trying to camouflage the fear poking at her.

"Maddie, there's something I need to say." This time he stopped and spun about to face her, standing only inches away. "I know we haven't known each other long."

Listening intently, her heart stuttered to beat normally.

"I want to keep seeing you when we return to San Diego."

Her breath hitched in her throat.

"But I think you should know ..."

This time she actually held her breath.

"I think I'm falling in love with you."

All the air in her lungs swooshed out in a long breath as she threw her arms around his neck. Up until five minutes ago she'd thought the same thing. But when her heart thought he was going to say something to tear them apart, she knew she wasn't just falling, she was full-fledged, no-holds-barred, in love with Dan O'Neil.

CHAPTER FOURTEEN

"**I** can't believe you've lived in San Diego all these years and have never been to the zoo."

Maddie shrugged a shoulder. "What can I tell you? I didn't have a handsome Marine Biology PhD candidate to show me the errors of my ways."

"That may be, but still I would have bet serious money you would at least have come to see the pandas. Especially since there are only four zoos in the country with a giant panda exhibit."

"Hey, if one of them wasn't in the market for a new house …" She trailed off, smiling up at him, still struggling to believe how far they'd come in so little time.

When she'd left Kona a few short weeks ago, she hadn't had the slightest idea what she was getting herself into dating a retired naval officer on a path to a doctorate degree. The man made a Swiss watch look disorganized and undisciplined. By the end of her first week back in San Diego, Dan had updated the virus and malware programs on her computer and tinkered with her laptop so it ran faster than when she'd bought it. The second week, with her permission, he'd reorganized the kitchen cabinets to make the small space more efficient. Which it did. She was pretty sure soon he'd be color-coding her closet. And she loved every minute of it. Every minute with him. By the third week, she'd implemented a new policy of no work after 6:00 p.m. and they'd fallen into a steady routine, including after-dinner walks, each decompressing from their day. For a near civilian, Dan still did some serious working out every morning at the gym and prepping for the upcoming months kept him busy by day, but the evenings were for them. And much to her surprise, her clients accepted the change without complaint. All in all, her world had become a much better place.

Dipping quickly behind Dan, Maddie avoided colliding with a couple of pint-size kids running circles around their oblivious parents. "Who knew so many people can take off from work and come to the zoo on a Wednesday afternoon."

"You think this is crowded, you should see the park on the weekend." Dan took her hand and followed the signs to Koalafornia. "After we see the new exhibit, we'll stop for something to eat. Sound good?"

Maddie nodded. He could have suggested a snake pit for their next stop, and she would have happily agreed.

Approaching the cluster of totem poles at the exhibit entrance, a strained whimper had Maddie pausing to survey the surrounding area. The sound came again, and this time Dan heard it, recognizing its direction immediately. "Over there." He pointed.

A little boy, no more than two or three, stood amid a thatch of plantings across the walkway, quietly crying. Changing trajectory, she and Dan crossed the path to the small child. Maddie keeping an eye open for a parent or older sibling. Signs of someone frantic over a lost boy.

"I don't see anyone who could be searching for him," Dan said. Months ago Maddie had stopped asking herself how they seemed to be thinking the same thing so often and merely accepted that anything is possible with the right person.

Squatting down on her haunches, she extended her hand. "Hi there, little one."

Big water-filled brown eyes looked up at her, and Maddie actually put her hand to her heart, at the gripping little face.

"What's your name?"

The boy didn't respond, but he stared at her with such intense curiosity that he seemed to forget all about crying.

"I'll check in with someone in charge." Dan sprinted down the path and entered the nearest building.

"I'm Madeleine." Disappointed the little boy wasn't

saying anything and thrilled he'd at least stopped crying, Maddie inched closer. "Are you looking for your mama?"

"*Mahmum.*"

While she wasn't an expert in toddler speak, she was guessing that was the same as *Mama*. She extended her hand to wipe at the tears on his cheek, and, to her surprise, he walked straight up to her, put his hands by her neck and tried to climb onto her already wobbly lap. Slipping her arms underneath him, she tried to push to her feet.

The little guy grabbed on to her hair for leverage and pushed higher onto her lap. Maddie knew she was going to land flat on her butt, when a warm hand landed on her shoulder, steadying her.

"Easy there." Dan helped her to her feet, and she remembered so vividly the first time she'd looked into those captivating green eyes in the L.A. airport. Back then he'd also stopped her from falling on her flat on her backside.

A uniformed security guard stood behind Dan, speaking into a cell phone. Or maybe it was a walkie-talkie. "That's right. Opposite the Queenslander House."

Dan kept one arm around the small of Maddie's back while she propped the lost little boy on her hip.

"You do that quite well." He ran his other hand through the child's silky hair.

"You're thinking of Carolyn." It wasn't a question.

"When she was this age, I was still pretty much a kid myself."

Maddie nodded. Even though they both knew that age wouldn't come between her and Dan, she was still working on helping him to embrace that neither being over forty nor a retired naval officer were necessarily stepping stones to the nursing home.

"*Mijo.*" A short woman with jet-black hair, and an entourage of at least a dozen adults and children, came running up the hill.

"*Mahmum,*" the little guy repeated, this time flinging his arms outward and almost falling out of Maddie's grip.

"Oh, Mikey." The woman pulled him into a tight embrace and shifted to face Maddie. "I can't thank you enough for finding him. And I can't believe how far he walked, and no one noticed he was alone." The woman blew out a long breath.

"See, I told you he'd be fine," A teenage boy said with more confidence than showed on his face.

"You, I'll deal with later. Help Aunt Reina with the rest of the children."

The sullen teen turned to another dark-haired woman who must be his aunt, and began corralling the small group of children.

"Again, I can't thank you and your husband enough. God bless you." Flashing a steadier smile, the lady turned around, shouting instructions to one of the others in their group.

Dan stared off momentarily at the departing mother's back. "That had a nice sound to it."

"What had a nice sound to it?"

"*Husband.*" Dan spun about, took hold of her hand and began walking down the hill.

Pointing over her shoulder at the Koala viewing area behind them, Maddie sputtered, "I thought you wanted to see the koalas?"

"Changed my mind." He ducked off the paved path and led Maddie a few more feet around a large oleander bush in bloom. "I'd had other plans for the rest of our day, but somehow this seems right. Since the first moment you slammed into me, I've known you were someone special. It hasn't taken long to learn I want you in my life for always."

He placed his hand in his pocket, dropped to one knee and withdrew a small square black box.

Maddie's hand lifted to her open mouth.

"Madeleine Harper, you are the love of my life. Would you do me the honor, bestow upon me the greatest pleasure, and marry me?"

She wasn't sure what protocol was in a situation like this, but throwing herself on him and stealing a sloppy wet kiss seemed totally appropriate. Knocking him over and landing in the dirt hadn't been her plan, but she didn't care. Kissing him for all she was worth, she pulled away and mumbled yes, oblivious to the applause and cheers from the growing crowd on the path.

The same security guard who had helped with the missing child came over to them. "I'm sorry, but you're not allowed off the paved path."

"I know." It wasn't like Dan to break the rules. "But I couldn't wait." He slid the ring on her finger, and the crowd erupted again behind them.

The security guard smiled. "I suppose, once in a while, every rule needs to be broken."

Getting up first, Dan helped Maddie to her feet. Returning to the path, he slid his arm around her, and she snuggled into the crook of his shoulder.

"Who shall we call first?" he asked.

Lifting her head to look at him, they both echoed, "Carolyn."

Pulling out his phone from his pocket, he glanced down at Maddie. "Are you thinking wedding in Kona?"

She nodded. With her parents planning a move to Hawaii, and Dan's daughter living there, family wouldn't have to travel to share the day.

He tapped the screen. "Honeymoon in Maui?"

"How about Kentucky?" She settled her hand on his chest. "I've always wanted to see horse country."

Phone to his ear, listening to the ringing, Dan's eyes widened.

"Don't look so surprised. As long as we're together, anyplace is paradise."

EPILOGUE

"Have you ever seen anything more romantic?"

Alone on her brother Nick's veranda, arm in arm, Maddie and her new husband swayed to a tune no one else could hear.

Ava Everrett considered turning on the stereo and opening the patio doors so there's be a reason for them to dance, then again, "You know what they say about making your own music."

"Yes, there is that." Maile nodded at her daughter, then took a quick glance at the dancing couple just as Dan twirled his bride about and pulled her in close against his chest. Smiling wide Maile's nodded at her daughter. "There is definitely that. I'd better go see about the cake."

Taking a sip of champagne, Ava had to wonder how surrounded by so many people finding true happiness, all she'd found was a waste of time.

"They really do make a wonderful couple." Angela came up beside her sister-in-law. "Surprised the heck out of me. Not that Dan had proposed, but how fast they decided to get married."

Billy sidled up to his wife and handed her a ginger-ale. "When it's right it's right."

"That's what they said." Kara took a spot beside Ava.

Nick slid an arm around his wife. "Couldn't argue with them. When they said they wanted a small, family affair, your mother," Nick waved at Billy, "said no problem. And here we are."

Ava wasn't at all surprised her mother, the consummate romantic, had managed to throw an intimate and lovely wedding together in less than a week. They'd had a brief ceremony at the little wedding chapel on the beach, and a handful of friends and family, gathered at Nick's for the small reception. Of course, Maile Everrett had learned a few tricks from Lexie's mother, but still. The cozy ambiance was all Ava's mom.

"Here they come." Nick pointed his chin in his sister's direction.

Ava looked up and couldn't help but smile. Everyone around her looked so darn happy.

"You're seriously going to Kentucky for a honeymoon?" Billy asked.

Nick shook his head. "You do realize how many islands there are less than an hour away that any number of people would kill to honeymoon at?"

In a wispy blush colored, three quarter length dress, Maddie splayed her hand across her husband's chest and her cheeks flushed a sweet rosy shade as she looked up to meet his gaze, and smiled.

Dan's hand pulled his bride impossibly closer into his side and the simple gesture and sheer adoration in his eyes made Ava wonder why she'd taken so long to smarten up and dump her newly ex-boyfriend.

"My family is throwing a small reception for us there," Dan explained.

"Besides," Maddie looked to her brother. "Paradise isn't always a place."

"No," The bride's brother kissed his wife's temple. "No it's not."

Carrying a small two tiered cake that Yvette Harper had baked with a simple heart-shaped topper, Maile Everrett called everyone into the dining room and set the cake on the table.

While the others meandered to the other room as instructed, Emily sidled up beside her sister. "You haven't told mom you dumped the moocher yet, have you?"

Out of habit Ava started to say he wasn't a moocher and then realized there was no need to defend him anymore. "I haven't had the chance to mention it."

"Chicken."

She didn't bother to deny it, or hide a smile. "Maybe."

"So she doesn't know you're considering moving back home?"

Ava shook her head. She still hadn't completely made up her mind if leaving Honolulu was the right thing.

The small crowd gathered in the other room erupted in cheers and Ava smiled at the newlyweds. Resplendent in his dress whites, Dan gulped down the massive chunk of cake Maddie had struggled to pop into his mouth. She softly said something that looked like 'sorry' to him and then smiling at her, he carefully placed a much smaller morsel of cake into her open mouth and kissed the tip of her nose. Like her mother had said, so romantic.

Maybe Ava's first mistake years ago was not having paid more attention to those handsome navy buddies who'd always come home for a little R & R with her brother. Watching the most recent union of happy bride with equally elated military man, Ava had to wonder if maybe Billy didn't have a few more friends left.

EXCERPT FROM

LOVE BY DESIGN

All those years of hard work and making coffee were about to pay off. Big time. Ava Marie Everrett stood in the oversize boardroom of Emerson & Smythe Architectural Designs International in Honolulu, ready for *the* announcement.

Stanley Smythe Jr. sauntered into the conference area, bypassed the three male coworkers standing nearby and, on his way to the front of the room, waved a hand at the bottles stacked on the side table. "Ava, dear, why don't you help pour the champagne?"

"Certainly, Mr. Smythe."

For ten years she'd been paying her dues, working her way up the architectural corporate ladder. The last three of which she'd watched one career-making opportunity after another get assigned to a different brilliant and innovative architect. Each one with a Y chromosome.

"Let me give you a hand." Her colleague and friend, Greg Austin, shook his head at the cheap brand of sparkling wine and popped the first cork. "Looks like Sacramento is in the bag. This one has to be yours."

Accepting the opened bottle from Greg, she blew out a long steadying breath. "It was a team effort."

"Oh, come on. Every step of the way your ideas took the lead. The team knows, if E&S wins this—and I see no reason for a champagne toast if they haven't—the museum will be your baby. They couldn't have won the contract without you."

A small part of her wanted to scream to the world, "Yes. This is my baby." Over the last weeks just about each member of the team had, in one form or another, agreed with Greg that, this time, there was no way the archaic-thinking heads of E&S could pass Ava by for chief architect. Her style and flair were all over these drawings.

Months ago, when she'd learned that E&S had been selected to submit a design for the Sacramento Cultural Arts Museum, she'd begun pitching to be part of the team. The anchor building for the new multibillion-dollar Arts District, intended to rejuvenate the west side of the capital city, had consumed her thoughts. Visions of natural stone, indirect lighting and works by native artisans had taken over not only her every waking moment but her dreams as well. By the time the team members were announced, and she was counted among them, she could already feel the angles and lines of the sleek final structure oozing from her fingertips, like Spider-Man's webs.

One by one her associates and most of the support staff came by to collect a glass of the bubbly. The last open bottle poured and her own drink in hand, she scooted quickly to one side, away from the table, Greg on her heels.

"At least he didn't have the gall to ask you to serve the drinks as well."

She almost laughed at that. "Don't kid yourself. The words are probably on the tips of old Stanley's lips."

"Not even he would ask the newest chief architect to serve the champagne."

Chief architect. She really liked the sound of that. Any minute now Ava expected to hear the official announcement of the submission status and the naming of the lead personnel. Excitement bubbled inside her like the champagne in her flute. As chief architect she'd be working with the chief engineer on-site for much of the project. It took all she had not to grin like an overworked mother with the single winning Powerball ticket.

Only a few months ago Ava had unloaded the demanding lump of a man she'd wasted four years of her life on. Now that she had no one to tether her to Honolulu, Ava was free to take on the most demanding of projects anywhere in the world, without feeling an ounce of guilt. And this project was *the* one.

Greg shifted around, leaning in more closely. "Rumor has it that the delays in the Paris project have a few people here worried about their necks."

Now that was something Ava hadn't heard. But then again, not holding her liquor well, she rarely spent her free time in places conducive to garnering valuable tidbits of gossip. Not to mention she was missing the key body part to be accepted as one of the boys.

"As a matter of fact," he continued, "the backlash is so far spread that Emerson & Smythe has not been invited to submit for the Bay Area Aquarium."

"Really?" The engineering problems in the Paris project made up only the most recent black eye in a string of delays in the E&S portfolio. The elder Stanley's attention hadn't been on the business in years. Cutting corners to afford divorce number three was one of the reasons the man had been asked to retire.

A sly smile tugged at one side of Greg's face. "I've decided to accept a spot with Stevens, Orbach and Madison."

Holy cow.. SO&M was one of the biggest architectural and engineering firms in the world. "Chicago?"

Greg bobbed his head, grinning. "We'll keep the condo here in Honolulu, so Allison has a place to escape to if the snow gets taller than her."

"You'll be missed." She would certainly miss him. Greg was one of the few architects on the design teams even close to her age and the only one who never treated her like a glorified errand girl.

Stanley Smythe Jr. stood up front, tapping his glass with a spoon, as Greg clinked glasses with Ava. "Here it comes."

The bright grin on the new CEO's face outshone the bald expanse at the top of his head. "I'm sure you're all aware of why we're having this impromptu little morning celebration, but allow me the pleasure of confirming. Emerson & Smythe has been officially awarded the contract for the Sacramento Cultural Arts Museum."

Expected applause erupted, and Ava's heart hammered to the same rapid staccato.

"This project holds great importance to the firm. The competition was stiff, but we held every confidence that our brilliant and innovative team would come through for us. And they have."

Another burst of applause filled the room, and Ava closed her eyes, waiting for the sound of her name.

"For this reason we have chosen an exceptional team member, whose flair for the innovative shines through every time."

A smile pulled at her cheeks.

"Please join me in congratulating Brad Cummings."

Shock stabbed her. Bubbling excitement succumbed to a sour churning in her stomach. Putting forth her best effort, Ava plastered on her I'm-very-happy-for-you smile and silently hoped the *exceptional and innovative* architect's upcoming project imploded.

"I'm sorry, Ava." Greg looked as pained by the announcement as she was.

They'd done it to her again. "Yeah" was all she could say.

"I'd hoped, with old man Smythe stepping down, that maybe …"

Right. Maybe. She couldn't muster a reply. She'd had the same hopes. Out with the old and stuffy. In with the new and visionary. Except her hopes had just been shipped off to California without her. Disappointment filled her to the point she feared, if she opened her mouth, it would spew across the room with the force of a fire hose, and smack Brad and their boss in the face. Or maybe lower.

Greg turned his back, nudging her closer to the corner, and lowered his voice. "Maybe it's time you thought about moving on as well." With a casual shrug and a slow sip of his mimosa, he let the words sink in, before stepping back. "I've got a lot of files to start transferring. Think about what I said."

And just like that, Ava stood alone in the corner of the massive boardroom, while yet another male teammate received the moniker of chief architect, congratulatory slaps on the back, and a first-class ticket to Sacramento.

It had taken her four years to realize she was in a dead-end relationship with the *so* wrong guy. Maybe the fact that it had only taken her three years to realize the same thing about her job meant she was making progress. She deserved better than this. She deserved Sacramento. Setting down her morning cocktail, Ava worked her way across the room, stopping for a pat on the back as part of the winning team, along with a few regretful gazes from those who understood she'd been robbed.

Moving beside Brad at the front of the room, she offered the expected congratulations.

For a moment she thought she saw a flicker of apology in his eyes, but it passed so quickly that she was sure she'd only imagined it.

"Thanks. This is everyone's win."

She bobbed her head. After all, what was true in kindergarten still worked today. If she can't say anything nice, don't say anything at all.

Just as she shifted to approach the new president of E&S, the well-dressed man turned to her. "Wonderful news, isn't it?" And then the idiot handed her his empty glass. "Be a dear and fetch me a cup of coffee instead."

After years of being the only architect in the room asked to fetch coffee or bagels or to pick up lunch, she almost reached for the glass out of sheer habit. *Almost.* "I don't think so. Perhaps Brad here can help you."

For a few seconds her boss looked completely stunned, and then, as though struck by an unexpected wave of reality, the grin slipped from his face. "I know you put in your share of hours on this, and, rest assured, we're keeping that in mind for next time."

Next time. She leaned into her boss and whispered near his ear. "There won't be a next time." Stepping back and angling for the corridor, she leveled her shoulders, lifted her chin and raised her voice. "The next time *this* bright and innovative architect designs a bid-winning building, she won't be working for your cheap pocket."

Walking out the door and down the hall, Ava could hear Stanley Smythe Jr. sputtering in her wake.

"Who … What … Well."

Taking her phone from her pocket, she found the number for the Diamond Head Corner Coffee Shop. "Morning. Could you please deliver one hundred pounds of your French roast coffee to Emerson & Smythe?"

"One hundred pounds?"

"That's right. Oh, and include one of your single-serve coffeemakers. From now on the new president will be making his own blasted coffee."

Bright lights from cameras of every size and shape flashed in John Maplewood's face, right up to the minute his date's long legs slid from the backseat of the car. Bridget may not be an actress or model, but she certainly knew how to make an entrance. Or, in this case, an exit. All attention turned to the slit of the bright red dress that cut halfway up her thigh. The soles of her shoes matched exactly. Louboutin.

Had his brain cells not been fried after a four-hour conference call with Belgrade until the crack of dawn, he might have realized his offer to pay for tonight's outfit to excuse the short notice would cost him. The downside of the women in his life knowing his net worth kicked him in the gut once again. Just another reminder of what the female gender really wanted from him. Not that they objected to his looks or attention, but it always came down to the money.

"Mr. Maplewood." A good-looking guy from the local TV station shoved a microphone in John's face. "Rumor has it donations for this evening's fund-raiser have already topped last year's. Care to make an official announcement?"

His assistant Evelyn's words replayed in John's ear: *Make nice with the media. Remember it's all for the children.*

"I don't know any more than you do." John scoured his mind for the man's name. Started with an *M*. Michael. That was it. "But I certainly hope your source is right, Michael. This evening is all about the children."

Bridget leaned into John's side, gazing up at him, like an adoring pedigreed puppy—or at least in those shoes, a mutt impersonating a pedigree.

"FJM Global is proud to sponsor this wonderful event," he continued, ignoring Bridget's award-worthy performance. "And we look forward to the day when lymphoblastic leukemia is no longer in our vocabulary."

The reporter looked less than thrilled. Whether it was because this guy wasn't about to get the scoop on the night's numbers early or because John may have botched the guy's name, John wasn't sure. Either way, more superstars arrived and Mr. TV, having gathered what little gossip he would get from John, eagerly moved on to fresh fodder.

Inside the historical five-star hotel, the orchestra played a gentle rendition of a favorite Sinatra tune.

Bridget swayed to the music. "I love this song."

Across the dance floor, John spotted their table with a few of the biggest donors and their wives. John would be expected to cajole them into happily parting with their money. And he would. He'd kiss their feet and polish their shoes, if it would help eradicate this horrible disease. Next to the empty chair—that waited for him—sat Stanley Smythe, the elder, and his new bride. Why was it the older a rich man got, the younger the trophy wife? But worse, Smythe could talk the ear off a mule. Surely waiting a few more minutes before John started shoe-polishing wouldn't hurt. "Let's dance."

Bridget curled into his arms. "How did I win the lottery?"

"Excuse me?"

"I haven't heard from you in months. Then, out of the blue, with less than twenty-four hours' notice, I get an invitation to the black-tie event of the year."

He avoided meeting her eyes. This wasn't an evening of

wine and romance. It was business. Lifesaving business. "You love black-tie events."

"I do." She beamed. "Thank you."

Glancing down, he took note of her sincere smile. At least he thought it was. They'd met in court, when he'd been called as an expert witness. She'd wiped the floor with the opposing counsel. Bridget was a smart girl, and he'd enjoyed her company. Her sweet smile might have been enough to delude him into thinking she really cared for him—the man, the person—but, deep down, he knew, if he were a poor plumber, she wouldn't give him the time of day. On her birthday they'd only been dating a couple months. His assistant, Evelyn, had helped him pick out a beautiful 22K Italian gold etched bracelet for Bridget. The disappointment in her eyes, when she opened the blue velvet box, had cut him to the core. At first he didn't understand, and then it hit him. When they'd played tennis at the club with his friends, Bridget had admired one of the wives' bracelet. It's what had given him the idea for Bridget's birthday gift. But his friend's bracelet had been encrusted with diamonds. A rather extravagant expectation for only two months of casual dating.

Not that it mattered. He was done playing the game. But Evelyn had insisted, like Richard Gere in *Pretty Woman*, that business disguised as social events needed to be handled in pairs. Since John had given up dating, and his breakup with Bridget had been friendly, she was his best possibility. Besides, he doubted he'd have Richard Gere's luck hiring a working girl from Sunset Boulevard.

MEET CHRIS

Author of dozens of contemporary novels, including the award winning Aloha Series, Chris Keniston lives in suburban Dallas with her husband, two human children, and two canine children. Though she loves her puppies equally, she admits being especially attached to her German Shepherd rescue. After all, even dogs deserve a happily ever after.

More on Chris and her books can be found at www. chriskeniston.com.

Follow Chris on facebook at ChrisKenistonAuthor or on twitter @ckenistonauthor.

Join Chris' newsletter! Enjoy inside peeks and photographs from Chris' world and stories. Some times she'll thank her subscribers with a free copy of a new 99 cent flirt.

Please, if you enjoyed reading The Look of Love, consider helping other readers find the Aloha Romance series by taking a moment to leave a review. Reviews are a blessing to authors and readers alike. Even just a few words will do! Thank you.

www.ingramcontent.com/pod-product-compliance
Lightning Source LLC
Chambersburg PA
CBHW030840200726
48285CB00007B/2499